RAVENITE

VENGEANCE AND VAMPIRES BOOK ONE

ALICIA RADES

Published by Crystallite Publishing LLC.
Produced in the United States of America.
Edited by Megan Linski.
Cover design by KnesArt.

To Paul, who has never stopped believing in me.

1

———

Vampires are easier to kill after you've pecked their eyes out. This vamp was dangerously close to finding out exactly what that felt like.

I grabbed a fistful of his shirt and shoved the vampire up against the side of a brick building. He was at least four inches taller than me, but I easily matched his strength.

The darkness of night blanketed the damp, narrow alleyway. Humidity hung in the air from the recent rain, carrying the scent of putrid garbage over to us from the dumpsters nearby. Brick buildings rose on either side of us. Each was two stories high, with restaurants, bars, and the occasional boutique shop on the lower levels and apartments on the upper. I never ventured into this part of town during the day, but this street crawled with vampires at night. I was a sucker for vampires looking for a stake through the heart. They usually found it.

"Tell me where the Soulless are hiding!" I demanded.

The vamp's canines elongated until fangs protruded from

his mouth. "Look, lady," he said, showing them off. "I'm not scared of you."

Lady? Who the hell does he think I am?

"If you knew who I was, you'd be scared," I snarled.

"I'm a Soulless. I have no reason to be scared of you." He raised his left hand and pulled back his sleeve to prove a point. The mark of the Soulless was carved into his wrist—the same mark I'd noticed from my perch atop the bar's roof. The scar was shaped like a *V*, with two dots in the middle, one atop the other—fang marks.

"You should be the one who's scared," he threatened.

Okay, maybe he had a point. The Soulless scared me shitless, but Fangs here seemed harmless enough—for a vampire.

"I don't play games." My fingers tightened around his throat. "I could snap your neck right here, right now."

Fangs scoffed. "That ain't gonna kill me, honey."

"It'd give me plenty of time to get the job done," I countered. "Now tell me where to find your friends."

"What do you want with them?" he asked, narrowing his silver eyes at me.

"It doesn't matter," I said. "All that matters is that you're dead if you don't tell me."

Laughter bubbled up from his throat, and I nearly gagged at the scent of copper and vodka on his breath. Vampires didn't have to breathe, but it must've been habit. "You'll only consider killing me once I tell you."

Poor guy. He won't know what hit him.

"You obviously don't know who I am." I had a reputation to uphold, which meant if he didn't talk, he most certainly would die.

"*Should* I know you?" Fangs said with a suggestive smile.

Pig.

I slammed my fist into the side of his face for that one. He fell from my grasp and stumbled sideways but stood straight up again in less than a second. His lip was split where my knuckles connected with it, but like all vampires, he didn't bleed. The wound would heal within the hour, though.

"All I know, lady, is that you're in trouble," Fangs sneered.

Before I had a chance to respond, he lunged forward. A sudden sharp pain shot across my thigh. It felt like I'd just been impaled by a freaking sword. Was it forged in the fires of Hell or something? My leg felt like the flesh was burning off it.

I cried out and fell onto one knee. When I glanced down at my leg, I saw it was only a pocket knife.

Only a pocket knife. And it was sticking three inches into my flesh.

Lovely. I'd paid a high witch three months' worth of wages to enchant this outfit to shift with me, and now I'd forever have this hole in my jeans. My favorite pair of jeans, too. My ass looked perfect in them.

A moment of lust crossed Fangs's eyes as he stared down at the blood rushing out of my wound.

Yeah, that's right. I'm a shifter, I wanted to yell. *I bet I taste fan-freaking-tastic, you jackhole!*

I ripped the knife from my skin and pressed my free hand to my leg to slow the bleeding. Either Fangs had enough to drink earlier or he saw the fury etched into my face and thought better of sticking around, because after only a moment of hesitation, he turned and hightailed it down the alley.

A string of curse words trailed after him. It took me a moment to realize I was the one shouting them. I pulled my arm back and hurled the knife at his back, but it flew past his right hand, missing him entirely.

I was *not* done with this vamp. I rushed to my feet, ignoring the pain shooting up and down my leg and the blood soaking into my jeans. I was two steps from tackling him when a figure sprang out from the shadows. He slammed into Fangs's side and knocked him to the ground. I stopped in my tracks. The newcomer scurried to his feet and smashed a foot into the vamp's gut before he had a chance to move.

Oh, good. He's on my side.

I took a moment to steady myself against the side of the building and pressed my hand back over the wound. It burned more than it should, which could only mean one thing. The knife had been laced in vampire venom. Which meant I didn't have long before the blaze hit full force and I was down for the count.

"Cowen, you bastard!" the new guy shouted. His fist connected with Fangs's face.

Good shot, I thought. Except…

"Hey," I snapped. "I'm not some damsel in distress. I've got this."

The new guy was tall—at least six foot—with short black hair the same color as his skin. With those broad shoulders and all that muscle, he was the living embodiment of the phrase *tall, dark, and handsome*. I might've gone weak in the knees at the sight of him if I wasn't already feeling unsteady from the wound.

Handsome was too preoccupied with hauling Fangs to his feet that he didn't look at me when he replied. "No offense, but I need a moment with this vamp."

Wait. What?

"Uh, no," I objected. "He's mine."

Fangs grunted as Handsome shoved him up against the building in the same position I just had him in. Handsome landed another punch to his jaw with a loud *thud*.

"Hey!" I shouted. "Go easy on him. I need him to talk."

Handsome's striking brown eyes met mine, and they widened in shock. His gaze flickered down to my bleeding leg, and his face immediately fell. He hesitated for a moment, but it was one moment too long. Fangs swung his knee upward to connect with Handsome's groin. Handsome grunted and sank to the ground, while Fangs took off running.

I didn't waste a second. I sprinted after him. My leg burned like the sun, but I managed to put one foot in front of the other.

But Fangs was fast—faster than any human alive. It was one of the perks of being a vampire. Sure, vampirism had its drawbacks, like sensitivity to sunlight, bloodlust, and the fact that they couldn't breed the traditional way, but it also came with flawless beauty, quick healing, supernatural strength, and super speed at least five times faster than a normal human. Not to mention immortality—or at least a killer anti-aging enchantment. There were very few things that could kill a vampire. Luckily for me, I was pretty good at it.

I stumbled forward, and my hands slapped on the sidewalk. I caught myself and hurried back to my feet. The throbbing had spread down to my ankle and up my hip. I couldn't feel my knee anymore.

Chasing him on foot was useless.

I paused on the deserted sidewalk, only long enough to shift. Within seconds, my body shrank to the size and shape of a raven. Shifting didn't help the searing pain burning through my body. In fact, it only made it worse. But in my raven form, I didn't have to put weight on my leg. I shot into the air and flew down the street at top speed. My eyes caught the vamp turning down another alleyway up ahead.

I pumped my wings harder, but I'd lost my visual on him. I flew so fast around the turn into the alley that I nearly missed it. I quickly corrected my flight, but by the time my eyes focused, the alley was empty. The burning pain reached my wings, and I struggled to continue flapping them. I shot out of the alleyway onto a busy street bustling with nightlife. My eyes flickered from face to face, but Fangs was nowhere to be seen.

Frick!

The pain was more unbearable than ever. My vision blurred, and my head grew fuzzy. I wasn't ready to give up yet, but I didn't have the strength to keep going.

Just my luck.

I turned down a quiet street away from the bars and restaurants and shifted back into my human form. I sank to the ground and rested my head against the closest building. A string of curse words escaped my mouth. This was the closest I'd come to a Soulless in two years, and I'd let him slip through my grasp.

The distinct scent of dog hit my nose, and a low growl met my ears. My eyes shot open, only to be met by a pair of dark brown eyes just inches from my own. A black coat of fur covered the creature's body.

My heart hammered. Vampires weren't the only ones with supernatural perks. As a shifter, I was as strong as a vampire, a heck of a lot stronger than I looked. Plus, the vamps' heightened sense of smell and hearing didn't work on shifters for whatever reason, which made it hella easy to sneak up on them. But none of those perks would help me now. With the venom pulsing through my veins, I didn't have the strength to fight off another shifter.

"Please. I—" I started.

My voice cut off when the black wolf rose to its hind legs. His body lengthened, and his snout shortened as he shifted back into human form, his fur shrinking into his skin. Handsome stood fully-clothed in front of me.

"You're hurt," he said breathlessly, kneeling to my level to inspect my injury.

I resisted his touch and kept my hand pressed over the wound. Sweat dripped down my face.

"We have to get you to a hospital." He reached for me.

"No," I groaned, my head lolling to the side.

"Yes, we do," Handsome argued, like I didn't have a choice. His arms folded around me.

"No," I said more clearly, pushing him away. "A hospital won't help. The knife was laced in vampire venom."

Handsome's jaw tightened, and he cursed under his breath.

"It's not enough to change me," I told him through labored breaths. "Just enough to hurt like hell." I didn't mention the part about its anticoagulant properties, which meant if I didn't get this wound taken care of soon, I was going to bleed out. A wound infected with vampire venom didn't just heal on its own. It required a vampire's saliva or a healing spell. Luckily, I had one of those. I just had to get to it.

"Let me help you," he offered.

"I can do it myself," I protested. I pushed myself to my feet to prove a point, but I didn't have the strength to stay upright. I stumbled forward.

Handsome caught me before I smashed my face into the concrete below me. He smelled familiar, like cinnamon. It was the scent of my mom's kitchen on Thanksgiving morning... God, I missed her.

"You need help." He wasn't informing me; he was demanding.

There was no denying the truth, but...

"I don't know you," I said, harsher than I intended.

"I'm Venn," Handsome introduced. "And you?"

Yeah... I wasn't giving him my name.

"You're the Ravenite, aren't you?" Venn's voice was soft in my ear.

"Don't call me that." I drew away from him but only stumbled again. I had to do something *fast* if I didn't want to pass out.

"You are, aren't you?" he pressed.

Nausea twisted in my gut. I thought I might vomit from the pain. I only nodded as I sank to the ground and pressed my face into my bloody hands.

What's that healing spell again? I need to start memorizing these things.

"I have to call you something," Venn said. "If you don't want me calling you Ravenite, how about Rae for short?"

Close enough.

I nodded.

Venn knelt beside me. "Now that we know each other, will you let me help you?"

The sidewalk swayed in front of me. Unless I wanted to spend the night bleeding out here, I had no choice but to accept his offer.

"Okay," I agreed, though I was barely able to spit the word out. "No hospital, though. My apartment."

"No—" Venn began to protest.

"My apartment," I repeated, cutting him off.

Venn must've noticed the urgency in my tone, because he quickly scooped me into his arms. I gave him my address. Within moments, he was racing down the street, cradling me.

It wasn't like me to lead strangers back to my apartment, but I couldn't walk or fly, nor could I stay out on the street all night. I'd get home, heal myself, and figure the rest out later.

All I knew was that once I was back on my feet, I was going after that Cowen bastard.

It was my only choice if I ever wanted to see my sister again.

2

———

Venn burst through the door of my studio apartment and rushed across the room to the bed. I groaned in agony as he set me down. The feeling of the blanket on my skin was torture, as if I'd just been tossed onto a bed of needles. This was *so* not how I pictured things going the first time I brought a guy back to my place.

"Where's your med kit?" Venn demanded.

I tried to spit the words out through clenched teeth, but they wouldn't come. Instead, I pointed to my spell book on the table across the room.

"You don't have a first-aid kit?" Venn asked in disbelief.

I shook my head and pointed again.

His brow furrowed. "You want the book?"

I nodded, biting back a cry as the pain pulsed up my abdomen. "Now!"

We were running out of time. As Venn raced across the room for the notebook, I struggled to unzip my pants. There was no time for modesty.

"Help?" I asked desperately as soon as he returned.

Venn dropped the book next to me and began stripping my boots off. His fingers fumbled with the button on my jeans before he pulled them down my legs, careful not to touch my wound. Not that it mattered. Even the smallest touch sent a trail of fire across my skin. When he peeled my jeans back, it felt as if my skin was being ripped off with them.

"The book." I tried to point, but I could hardly lift my limbs.

Venn hurried to my side and flipped my spell book open.

"Page..." *Where was the spell again?* "In the middle somewhere."

"Tracking... Truth... Protection..." Venn read off the words I'd written in the headers of the pages.

"Keep going," I croaked out.

"Healing... Healing!" Venn stopped and scanned the page, then flipped to the next one. "Which one? There are a ton of them."

I struggled to sit up and somehow managed to prop myself up on my elbow. Venn turned the book toward me. The words swam in front of my eyes, and though I had perfect twenty-twenty vision, I squinted to see them more clearly.

"Next page," I told him.

Venn turned the page so quickly that he tore it a half inch. I cringed.

"There!" I cried.

I scanned the incantation. *Fantastic.* This was going to be one of the toughest spells I'd ever performed. I let out a shaky breath. Let's hope nothing went wrong. I began muttering the words under my breath.

Go away, pain! I thought to myself. Whoever said becoming a vampire was comparable to labor was insane. I was experiencing a mere taste of what vampire venom could do. If labor was even a fraction this bad, I was never having kids. And let's hope to *God* no vampire ever tried to change me.

I reached the end of the incantation, but the pain only burned more intensely. Had I made it *worse*? This spell was supposed to counteract supernatural injuries.

Where'd I get this crappy spell from anyway? I glanced at my notes in the header of the page. It came from one of my boss's clients, Mrs. Carlyle. She was the sweetest old lady you'd ever meet, but this wouldn't be the first time she sold us a shoddy spell.

What a bitch. Devin *had* to stop offering her money.

"Go back," I instructed though clenched teeth.

Venn flipped to the previous page.

This was a basic healing spell. I'd used it the last time a vamp tore a muscle in my shoulder, so I knew it worked, but it wouldn't do anything about the venom. That, I was going to have to ride out.

If I don't die first, I thought to myself. *Okay, here it goes.*

I pressed my hands to my wound. I could hardly open my mouth, but I pushed past the pain and whispered the incantation under my breath.

I can't die. I need to find the Soulless. I need to save my sister.

I couldn't explain how I knew Jenna was still alive after all this time, but I couldn't bring myself to believe she was dead. I'd felt a piece of myself die with my parents, but I hadn't felt that with Jenna yet. She was still out there somewhere.

I couldn't tell if the incantation took, so I recited it again. A sharp, stabbing pain shot down my leg and up my hip. The fire in my body filled my lungs, and I gasped for air.

This was it. I was going to die. My body was ripping into a million pieces, and there was no spell in the world that could piece me back together.

An earth-shattering scream filled the air around me, and then… nothing.

My mind swam through a fog as thick as syrup. I was vaguely aware I was still alive, but I couldn't seem to hold on to the memory of what had happened to me.

Where am I? I repeated to myself each time my mind cleared enough that I could manage a coherent thought. *Why does everything hurt so much?*

My mind slipped back into oblivion.

What felt like hours later—or days—I finally became aware of my body again. The light weight of a blanket settled over my legs, and the heavy, humid air left my skin slightly damp. A dull ache spread across my thigh.

"Ugh," a voice filled my ears. It took me a moment to realize the groan had come from me.

"Rae?" a second voice said softly.

Rae? That's a strange thing to call me. Only a moment later did I realize I'd told Venn to call me that.

My eyes shot open. I knew I was lying in my bed because of the ache in my back that I woke to every morning. The familiar water stain on the ceiling stared back at me.

"You're awake." Venn sat at the edge of my bed in my dining room chair. It was the only place to sit in my entire apartment.

The dull glow of morning light filtered in through the dusty window next to my bed. I struggled to push myself to a sitting position. The fire in my body had subsided, but my muscles hurt when I moved them, like I'd just finished running a marathon—and I wasn't a runner. My stomach twisted in hunger.

When my eyes landed on Venn's face, my hunger didn't seem to matter anymore. My stomach shifted for entirely different reasons. I'd invited this guy to take my pants off last night. *How embarrassing!* I mean, it was to save my life, but still…

I couldn't take my eyes off Venn, off his smooth skin and strong jaw. I wanted to throw my arms around his neck and drag him into bed with me.

It's the adrenaline from last night talking, I told myself. *You're acting weird because he helped you.*

"What?" Venn asked innocently. He'd *totally* caught me staring.

Of course he did! You're barely two feet from his face.

I didn't know what to say. "Have we met before?"

Venn shook his head. "Not that I remember, anyway."

"What are you still doing here?" I asked in barely a whisper. We were strangers, after all, and he'd been watching me sleep all night like a creep.

"I wanted to make sure you were all right," he replied.

Okay, so maybe he wasn't a creep. Maybe he was a gentleman. He'd draped a blanket over my exposed legs while I slept, so there was that.

"You're feeling better, aren't you?" Venn asked.

I lifted the covers to inspect my injury and was surprised to find a washcloth taped over the wound. The dry, crusted blood I expected to find wasn't there.

"I couldn't find a first-aid kit, so I had to improvise a bandage," he admitted.

The tension in my chest softened. "You cleaned it for me?"

"I did what I could."

My face heated at the thought of him tending to me while I slept. He could probably see the blush on my pale cheeks. I avoided his gaze and carefully peeled back the tape on my thigh. The washcloth dropped away to reveal that the wound had mostly healed, but a large, tender bruise remained. I pulled the covers back over my legs.

"Since you're okay now, I think I'll go." Venn lifted the chair and returned it to its spot at the table.

"Wait," I croaked out.

He paused and looked back at me. His eyes drooped, as if he hadn't slept all night.

I cleared my throat. "You're not going to turn me in, are you?"

His eyebrows drew together. "Turn you in?"

"Yeah, well…" I glanced around the tiny apartment, not really looking at anything—not that there was much to look at. I just couldn't manage to meet his gaze. "You know what I am. You know what I've done."

Venn inched his way across the room and shoved his hands into his jean pockets. "You mean that I know you're the Ravenite?"

I internally flinched at the word. I didn't deserve the respect that came along with the name. I was Rachel Collins, low witch and raven shifter in hiding. I was just a cashier at a spell shop who happened to kill vampires on her off-hours. But I wasn't special. I was barely an adult. I could hardly remember to do my own laundry, for heaven's sake! I wasn't the fierce, confident vigilante everyone thought the Ravenite was.

But I *was* the girl the police wanted.

"I've killed enough vampires to earn me a life sentence," I said.

As far as I was concerned, I was doing the police a favor by taking out vile vamps. *They* weren't going to kill them, not without a trial, at least. Some people still saw them as human. They called them *diseased*, but I'd seen enough to convince me otherwise. Vampires lost their humanity the moment they changed.

It wasn't like I had a grudge against vampires or anything. Okay, maybe I did. But I didn't kill just anyone. I only killed the ones who deserved it.

"Relax," Venn said. "I'm not going to tell anyone. The vampires are better off dead."

Exactly! Except Venn didn't say it with vengeance in his tone. He said it more like it was fact.

And let's face it, Venn was still a stranger to me. I couldn't just *trust* that he wouldn't out me. I was going to have to ditch Nocton and move to another city, preferably somewhere far away from Illinois where no one had ever heard the name *Ravenite*. It didn't matter where I went as long as there were vamps to slay.

Great. Bloodstone was the only place I'd ever manage to find a job that taught me anything about magic. Not to mention I was never going to find another place this cheap. I mean, it was a total dump, but at least I could afford it. I'd have to find a roommate.

Oh, God. Not a roommate.

Not to mention there was this Soulless guy running around now. I couldn't just walk away from that, not if I could use him to find Jenna.

Venn eyed me.

"What?" I asked innocently.

"I'm curious... how've you gone this long without getting caught?"

I shrugged.

Venn continued to stare at me, waiting for me to answer.

I wasn't interested in opening up to a stranger, but I had questions of my own to ask him, and it wasn't like he couldn't figure this one out on his own.

I sat up straight in bed and pulled the blanket around me. "I'm not registered as a shifter."

Venn raised an eyebrow. "Just a witch, then?"

I nodded.

"That was a pretty decent spell you cast last night," Venn pointed out. "You must be at least a mid-witch."

I shrugged again. "Somewhere between a low witch and a mid-witch. I'm still learning how to control my magic."

Venn bit his lip, like he wanted to say more but wasn't sure he should. I stared back at him with a questioning gaze.

"What were you doing with that vamp last night?" he asked.

Wait. Did he think I was just going to spill all my secrets because he helped me home?

"You already asked a question," I pointed out. "It's my turn."

Venn hesitated but eventually sank into the chair behind him, like he was settling in for a long conversation. "Fair enough."

My mind raced through fifty different questions at once. If we were going to play twenty questions, I had to make mine count.

"I want to know more about that vamp," I settled with. "You seem to know him."

"Not exactly," Venn said. "He stole something from me, and I tracked him down to get it back. What were *you* doing with him? You know he's a Soulless, right?"

"Yeah." *That was kind of the idea.*

Venn leaned forward in his seat and rested his elbows on his knees. "You know who the Soulless are, don't you?"

I scowled. "Of course I do. I'm not an idiot."

The Soulless were an elite group of vampires—*the* elite group. They were the ones created by Valkas, the original vampire. He showed up eight years ago at the same time magic appeared in our world. The Soulless were the worst of the vampires, the ones in Valkas's immediate circle. He left his mark on them when he changed them so that everyone would know to be afraid. Their mark was a warning. And there wasn't a soul in the world who wasn't afraid of them.

Except for me, of course.

I'm a terrible liar.

"If you knew he was a Soulless, what were you doing getting into a knife fight with him?" Venn asked.

Was Venn *mocking* me? He didn't deserve to know my whole life story. Then again, he'd found Cowen once already. Maybe he could help me find him again.

I swallowed hard. "He has something I need, too."

"What's that?" Venn's gaze bore into mine, challenging me to reveal more.

My teeth ground together. I *really* didn't like all these questions.

Venn leaned back in his chair when I didn't answer. "I don't know yet if you're friend or foe. What if we're after the same thing?"

Good point.

"You can relax," I said. "All I need from him is information."

Venn's expression hardened, and I thought I detected a

hint of concern in his tone. "You really don't want to mess with a Soulless."

I scoffed. "Says the guy who punched one in the face last night."

Venn crossed his arms. "Yeah, well, I had my reasons."

"So do I," I replied flatly. "Can you hand me my pants?"

"These bloody ones?" Venn rose from his chair and bent to the floor beside my bed.

"Yeah. They're my best pair," I said, reaching for them.

Venn averted his gaze as I pulled them on. I could only guess it was out of respect, but I kept the blanket draped over my legs, so it's not like he'd see anything even if he wanted to. After I was dressed, I pushed back the covers and hung my legs off the side of the bed.

"So," I said, running my fingers through my tangled black hair. "Now that we've established that we're friends, what's the plan?"

Venn furrowed his brow. "Plan?"

"Yeah." I rose to my feet.

My thigh protested since the spell was still working to heal it, but I'd endured worse. I crossed the room and grabbed the bag of bread next to the fridge. Venn's eyes followed me the whole time.

"Are we going after this guy or what?" I asked as I shoved a bland piece of bread in my mouth. I would've toasted it, but I was too hungry and impatient.

An expression of disbelief washed over Venn's face as he stepped into the small kitchen beside me. "*Go after*? As in, together?"

I nodded. If he didn't help me, I may have to wait years before I found another Soulless with answers.

"You know I'm good with vampires," I pointed out. "I'm a shifter. I'm strong—and fast."

"So am I," Venn said in a clipped tone.

I took a step back, holding up my bread up in surrender. "Right, I know. But don't we both stand a better chance together?"

"No," Venn said with conviction.

What? He didn't think I'd slow him down, did he?

"I can't let you get involved with someone like this," Venn said.

I let out a breath of disbelief. "I'm already involved!"

Venn pursed his lips. "Well, maybe you should get *un-involved.*"

I swallowed my final bite of bread and leaned against the counter. "I told you last night, I'm not some damsel in distress."

Venn opened his mouth to say something but only exhaled. After a moment of holding my challenging gaze, he finally spoke. "You're hurt. I don't want you to get hurt again."

He didn't even know me; he couldn't mean that.

"I can handle getting hurt," I said with my head held high. What I *couldn't* handle was letting this opportunity pass me by. "I'm going after him with or without you. You wouldn't want me to find him first, would you?"

Venn's teeth clenched. "You're going to be a problem no matter what I do, aren't you?"

I put on my best innocent face. "My friends don't call me *stubborn* for nothing."

I internally laughed at the mention of friends. I didn't have any friends—not anymore—but Venn didn't need to know that.

"How do I know I can trust you?" Venn asked.

A hundred versions of the answer flew through my head, so I was surprised by the words that actually left my mouth. "You don't."

I didn't exactly know if I could trust him, either. We were just going to have to take a chance on each other.

Venn stepped forward and narrowed his eyes at me. My backside was already pressed against the countertop, so I had nowhere else to go. My skin heated, and my mouth went dry. He was testing me, waiting for me to back down.

I won't.

"All you want from this guy is information?" Venn asked, his hot breath brushing across the top of my head.

"Yes," I stated without blinking, despite my racing heart.

How did this guy's challenging gaze send my heart hammering harder than it did when I stood up to a freaking *Soulless*?

"What kind of information?" Venn pressed.

"That's personal," I replied, refusing to answer. He was already objected to me getting involved with *one* Soulless. What would he think if I told him I intended to crash their hideout?

"Tell me again why I should help you," Venn insisted.

He was only inches from me now. Had this guy ever heard of a personal bubble? Not that my apartment left much room for personal space.

"Be—because," I stuttered.

Stupid mouth.

I cleared my throat. "Because I need your help."

No! That's not what I meant to say!

It wasn't like I could shove the words back down my throat.

Venn's expression softened, and he took a step back.

"I can help you, too," I said in a rush, standing up straighter. "I'm a witch, after all. I can perform spells, and—"

"Fine," Venn said with a heavy sign.

Wait. What?

"Really?" I asked, not quite sure I believed him.

"Against my better judgement, yes, I'll help you."

I jumped in excitement, startling Venn and sending a fresh wave of pain through my thigh. I quickly composed myself. "Cool. When do we start?"

"Whenever you're ready," Venn said.

I ran my fingers through the knots in my hair. "I'm ready. So… where do we find this guy?"

Venn shook his head. "It's not that simple. I think we should head back to my place first. We'll talk to the family and come up with a game plan."

I passed Venn and headed to my dresser to gather my purse and the few belongings I carried when I wasn't out getting myself into supernatural trouble.

"The family?" I asked without looking back. "You spend *one* night at my place, and suddenly I'm meeting your parents?" I turned from my dresser and slung my purse over my shoulder. "Sorry, Venn, but we may want to slow this relationship down a little."

Venn leaned his shoulder against the refrigerator and smirked at me from across the room. "To be fair, *you're* the one who invited me back to your place and had me take your pants off."

"Oh, God," I groaned, shoving my face into my hands. "That's how you're going to introduce me to your parents, isn't it? I'll never live it down."

"Relax," Venn said with a laugh. "You don't have to meet my parents. They're dead."

My entire body tensed at the words. It was official. I was the worst person on the planet. My hands slowly dropped from my face, and my mouth hung open. All I wanted to do was tell him that I knew how he felt, but my lips refused to move.

"Come on." Venn straightened and crossed the room toward the door. He acted so casual, like my comment hadn't bothered him in the slightest. "We should get going. Ryland's going to be mad enough at me as it is. The sooner he's done yelling at me, the sooner we can go after Cowen."

I grabbed my spell book off the table then followed behind Venn into the hall, flipping off the light and locking the door behind me. I bent and peeled back the loose baseboard in the hall next to my front door and placed my key inside the crack. It was easier to leave it there than coming up with the money to enchant it to shift with me.

"Who's Ryland, and why would he be mad at you?" I asked when I stood.

"You'll meet him soon, but be careful," Venn warned. "He'll be mad at me for bringing home a stray."

A stray? I almost asked before realization hit. *Me. He means me.*

This Ryland guy was going to be mad at *me*. Too bad he had no idea I was a fighter. And when I fought back, I fought back *hard*.

3

"Is there anything I should know before I meet your family?" I asked Venn once we reached his car. It was a black four-door sports car with a sleek, modern design. Though it looked at least a few years old, its paint shined as if it'd been recently cleaned. The car was parked a few blocks away next to the bar we'd both confronted Cowen outside of. The street was quiet, in stark contrast to the bustling nightlife of last night. "Anything that will help me make a good first impression?"

Not that I care.

Venn turned the air conditioner on full-blast before it had a chance to cool. Hot air burst from the vents and blew in my face. The air today was thick and far too hot for a summer morning.

Venn pressed on the gas, and the car sped forward with a quick jolt. This thing clearly had its fair share of horsepower. "You could've started with a better pair of pants."

"I told you these were my best pair," I defended. "You of all people should know how valuable clothes that shift with you are. Yours are obviously enchanted."

Venn glanced at my pants then back to the road. "They're that valuable?"

My brow furrowed. Was he toying with me, or did he really not know? Either he was made of a crap ton of money, or he was sleeping with a high witch. His car was nice, but it wasn't *that* nice. I had to guess it was the latter.

"Do you have a cleaning spell in that book of yours?" Venn asked, gesturing to the bag on my lap. "Something that will get rid of the blood?"

I scoffed. "Sure I do, but if I could actually perform the spell, don't you think I would've done something about that water stain on my ceiling?"

"I thought you said you were a mid-witch," Venn said.

"No," I corrected. "I said I was somewhere between a low witch and a mid-witch. There are some spells I can't get right, okay?"

"Whoa." Venn held up a hand in surrender. "I didn't mean to hit a nerve."

Had I been that harsh about it? *Woops.*

"It's okay," I told him in a softer tone.

I looked out the window as we turned down a residential street. The houses here were small and cramped together, but they looked well taken care of, which was in total contrast to the dump neighborhood I lived in. Here, the houses actually had a homey charm to them.

Venn pulled into the driveway of a white two-story home. A bright flowery wreath hung on the front door. My thoughts immediately went to Jenna. Every spring, we'd pull out craft supplies and make a wreath for Mom for Mother's Day. It would hang all year until we made her a new one. My heart ached at the reminder of my family.

"What's wrong?" Venn asked as he shifted into park. He sounded genuinely concerned.

My face must've gone pale—paler than normal. I shook my head, as if trying to rid the memory from my mind. "Nothing. It's just a lovely home."

Venn opened the door and stepped out of the vehicle. "Yeah, we got lucky."

I slung my purse over my body and followed behind him up the sidewalk. Nerves twisted in my gut. Sure, I had no problem confronting a Soulless in a dark alley, but something about voluntarily meeting new people was terrifying.

Venn led me inside. I warily stepped over the threshold into a narrow hallway. The first thing I noticed was the faint smell of cinnamon. It was the same scent I'd noticed on Venn, the smell of comfort, of home. Hardwood floor spanned in front of us, reaching back into the house where it met an open doorway that led to a bathroom. A flight of stairs rose to our right. Framed drawings hung on the wall and climbed upward with the steps. Two other doorways opened from the entryway, one leading to the living room on our left and the other to a dining room on our right. I noticed six chairs set around the table, so I figured Venn's family couldn't be *that* big. I hadn't had a chance yet to ask more about who lived here with him. If his parents weren't around, who did he live with?

"Venn Jason Michaels!" a deep voice boomed from upstairs.

A shudder traveled through my body. We were in trouble. Well, Venn was, and I'd walked straight into it. Part of me wanted to stay just to see the fight while another part of me felt like ducking out of the house the first chance I got. I kind of had a love-hate relationship with drama.

"I'm back!" Venn shouted before lowering his voice and gesturing to the living room. "You can set your stuff down in here."

I followed behind him and sank onto the couch, but I didn't accept his invitation to set my bag down. Instead, I held the strap close to my chest.

My eyes swept across the room. This room alone had more decor in it than my entire apartment, though it wasn't like my apartment was much bigger. A TV hung on the wall across from me, and a coffee table sat in the center of the room with a vase of flowers placed on it. A brick fireplace was built into the far wall, and a painting of a landscape hung above it. On either side of that stood two bookcases filled with old books and picture frames. I noticed a skinny redheaded teen girl in several of the photos and wondered who she was. Her pale skin was in stark contrast to Venn's dark complexion, so I guessed they weren't related.

Just as I thought it, the same redheaded girl rushed into the room. She stopped abruptly in the doorway, and her wide eyes locked on Venn. He faced the doorway with his arms crossed, bracing himself for whatever came next.

"Ryland's pissed," Red warned.

"I know," Venn replied tensely as heavy footsteps pounded down the stairs.

"Venn," the deep voice came again.

Red stepped aside as the man the voice belonged to stomped into the room. His facial structure was similar to Red's, but he had chestnut brown hair. He didn't look much older than me, yet he towered at least a foot above Red. If I thought Venn was made of muscle, he was nothing compared to this guy. His biceps were as big as the trunk of the tree my dad built my childhood treehouse in. In other words, the guy was *massive*.

"What happened—?" Tree Trunks started to say, but his voice cut off when his eyes fell on me. His jaw tightened. "Who's this?"

Venn raked his fingers through his hair and sighed. "This is Rae. I mentioned her last night."

"She's the *situation*?" Tree Trunks boomed in disbelief. He cursed under his breath and clenched his fists tight. He spun around and took a few paces—which basically covered the whole room with his long legs—before turning back to Venn. "You let Cowen get away for *her*?"

"I—"

"What did you *do* to her?" Tree Trunks cut Venn off and stared down at my bloody jeans.

I was stunned by the accusation.

"Nothing," Venn defended.

Tree Trunks shot him a look of disbelief.

I stood abruptly. "This was Cowen's doing. Venn saved me."

Tree Trunks hesitated for a moment, but he didn't reply. He turned back to Venn. "Why'd you bring her here?"

Venn's gaze darted between mine and Tree Trunks's. "She's on our side."

"So what?" Tree Trunks objected. "She's a complete stranger. You can't just bring strangers into our home. This is supposed to be a safe place!"

"She needs our help," Venn replied, calmer than I expected him to.

"You should've at least asked first," Tree Trunks insisted.

"Asked who?" Venn's voice rose. "You? You're not in charge here. Sondra would've—"

"It doesn't matter what Sondra would've done," Tree Trunks argued. "While she's gone, I *am* in charge."

This was getting to be too much. I was a sucker for violence, but only when it involved kicking vampire ass. I didn't want to be the reason this home turned into a war zone.

"Hey," I said to get their attention. All eyes turned to me, including Red's in the doorway. "All I need is—"

Tree Trunks held up a hand to stop me. "Hold on. I'll get to you in a minute."

"Excuse me?" I snapped. This guy was a total asshole. I knew it was his house and everything, but I couldn't just stand around and let him treat everyone like dirt.

Tree Trunks blinked at me, like he couldn't believe I'd objected to his orders.

"You interrupt people an awful lot," I observed. And I hadn't even known the guy for two minutes. "As I was saying, all I need is help finding Cowen. Venn offered his expertise. As soon as we find him, I'm gone."

Tree Trunks's jaw tightened. "This isn't about you. This is between me and Venn."

"Fine," I agreed. "Have your little chat, but you can't stop Venn from helping me."

"Believe me," Venn said with amusement on the corner of his lips. "She'd castrate you if you tried."

I smiled proudly, glad he understood me. I adjusted the strap on my purse and stepped out into the hall while Venn and Tree Trunks continued yelling at each other. I took a seat on the bottom stair, intent on waiting out their fight where I could still eavesdrop. Though at their volume, I could probably easily hear them halfway across the street.

"Hey," Red said as she sat next to me. "I'm sorry about Ryland. He's never like this. He's actually really sweet, and I say that as a sister who can't stand him half the time."

He could've fooled me.

"He's only mad because he's been up all night worrying about Venn," Red explained, keeping her eyes fixed on a hangnail she was fidgeting with. "Venn called to let us know he was okay, but Ryland couldn't help but worry, you know?"

My shoulders relaxed. It sounded like the time I was fifteen and snuck out of the house to attend a party. Jenna wouldn't take me because I was only a freshman, but I went anyway. We both got an earful from Dad the next morning.

"I'm Fiona, by the way," Red introduced.

I cleared my throat. "Rach—Rae. I'm Rae."

"Cool, so why—?"

"Back off, Ryland!" Venn's voice boomed from the other room, cutting Fiona off.

She glanced to the living room, looking positively embarrassed by the guys she lived with.

"You don't have to worry," Venn continued. "I'll take care of her."

Take care of me? Who says I need taking care of?

"That's not the problem," Ryland responded. "How do we know we can trust her?"

I raised my eyebrows at Fiona. "They're just going to keep talking about me like I can't hear them?"

Fiona crinkled her nose and nodded. "Probably."

"We *can* trust her," Venn emphasized. "Because…"

I couldn't see Ryland from the hall, but I pictured him crossing his arms when he spoke.

"Because...?" Ryland prompted.

"Because..."

Every muscle in my body tensed. *Oh, God. He's going to out me as the Ravenite. I know he said he wouldn't turn me in, but what if one of his friends does?*

Venn let out a frustrated growl. "I just trust her, okay? Isn't that enough?"

I relaxed. He was keeping my secret.

Venn lowered his voice, but I could still make out his words clear as day. "There's just... something in her eyes."

Ryland paused for a beat. "That doesn't give you the right to act without consulting us first."

Fiona turned to me, ignoring the on-going argument. "So, how'd you meet Venn?"

I still didn't know this girl—or Venn for that matter. I didn't know any of them, so I was hesitant on how much to say. I avoided her gaze, looking anywhere but her eyes—at the front door, at my boots, up the stairs at the sketches on the wall. Even though her question was innocent enough, I purposely didn't answer.

"Those are nice," I said flatly, gesturing to the closest drawing. Venn's eyes stared back at me from the paper. Whoever had drawn him had managed to capture the soft beauty in his eyes perfectly.

"Yeah," Fiona agreed. "Sondra drew them all."

I twisted further to view the portraits. I noticed a drawing of Fiona beside Venn's, and Ryland next to hers.

"Who's Sondra?" I asked.

"She's mine and Ryland's cousin," Fiona answered.

"So, you're all related?" I asked. "Even Venn?"

Fiona shook her head. "Not by blood. We sort of adopted Venn and Teagan."

"Teagan?" I asked.

"She's probably in her room listening to music to drown out the guys' argument." Fiona gave a light giggle, as if it was a common occurrence.

"You all live here together?" I asked.

It felt like there should be an adult in the house, until I realized *I* was an adult. *When did that happen?*

Another voice in my head quickly responded. *The day Mom and Dad died.*

"Yep," Fiona answered.

I eyed her curiously. She definitely looked younger than me. "How old are all of you?"

"Venn's nineteen, and Ryland and Teagan are twenty. I'm seventeen."

I was eighteen and couldn't afford a place a quarter this nice. How did they do it?

"Sondra owns the house," Fiona explained, like she could read my mind. "She's a lot older than the rest of us. She inherited the house from her parents and then took me and Ryland in when ours died."

"Oh," I said softly. It sounded like Sondra was running some sort of orphanage. I'd fit in perfectly.

Great. Because that was just the kind of place you wanted to fit in at.

An uncomfortable silence hung between Fiona and me, but Venn's and Ryland's voices in the other room somehow made it less awkward.

"So, what do you need to find Cowen for?" Fiona asked. "You don't seem like the kind of girl to get involved with people like him."

I laughed a deep, full-belly laugh I couldn't control. "You'd be surprised."

If my job was any indication, I was *exactly* the kind of girl to get involved with people like Cowen. Bloodstone wasn't exactly legal, and neither were my… hobbies.

Eight years ago, Valkas showed up and started changing a bunch of people into vampires, presumably recruiting them for his Soulless army—until the Soulless fell off the radar two years ago, not long after they kidnapped my sister as a blood slave. Anyway, when I was a kid, the new vampires went on killing sprees all across the US. No one knew for sure if it was the product of bloodlust or if it was under Valkas's orders. Maybe he just wanted to spark fear in the masses. Which, by the way, totally worked.

At the same time, ordinary people began to discover they had magic. Shifters started shifting, and witches started casting spells. It began with adults, but kids my age followed a few years later as we grew older. Magic usually appeared at first during times of high emotions, but the more we used it, the more we could control it. Most people never changed, but you never knew if you'd end up supernatural or not. It was clear from the beginning that shifter magic ran in families, but witch magic was random. There wasn't a genetic component that anyone knew of.

But of course, witches and shifters were lumped into the same supernatural category as the heartless, murderous vampires. A civil rights movement fought to treat all supernaturals as equals to humans. In a compromise, the government ruled that supernatural creatures couldn't be charged for what they were, only for the crimes they had committed.

Magic was outlawed except in special government-approved cases, and supernaturals were required to be registered as such. Blood banks were set up for vampires who'd already been changed so that they could satisfy their cravings without killing or changing more people. It was a great solution but a crappy deal. The government didn't even pay people for their blood, but they sure liked to charge vamps for it. And people bought into the whole thing out of fear, because at least there were fewer vampire attacks.

Obviously, however, if there are laws in place, people are bound to break them. Vampires continued to feed without consent, shifters continued to shift, and people like me continued to deliver justice in a world with a broken justice system. Magical objects and spells were sold on the black market for a pretty penny, which meant that if Bloodstone were ever discovered, I'd already have a decade or two in the slammer just for working there. If all my crimes were laid out on the table, I'd be in for life. But seriously, who's counting?

"Yeah…" I said to Fiona, dragging out the word as all these thoughts rushed through my head. "We probably shouldn't get into that."

"Hey," Ryland's clipped tone came from behind us.

Fiona and I both turned. The anger had melted from his face, but I still sensed something in his expression that told me he wasn't entirely pleased.

"You can stay for now," Ryland told me.

From beside him, Venn shot me a reassuring smile. I wasn't sure what he'd said to Ryland to change his mind, but I was grateful that he fought for me.

Ryland's eyes flickered down to my thigh. "Find her a clean pair of pants, Fiona. Teagan should have some that'll fit her."

"I can try," Fiona said, "but you'll have to wish me luck getting anywhere *near* Teagan's closet."

"Good luck." Ryland didn't sound the least bit genuine. "Just be quick. We're leaving in ten minutes."

My brow furrowed. "Leaving where?"
Ryland's jaw tensed. "To get Cowen."

4

When Fiona said we'd have a hard time getting into Teagan's closet, I pictured walking into a blonde bimbo's glittery pink bedroom. Imagine my surprise when we entered her room just in time for a knife to whizz past my head. The blade hit the wall beside me with a *thud*.

I jumped back from the door, my heart racing.

"Tea," Fiona scolded, ripping the knife from a board screwed into the wall. Every inch of the board was filled with nick marks. "Are you *trying* to scare our guest away?"

Teagan eyed me from across the room. She was strikingly beautiful, with tan skin, high cheekbones, and full lips. Her dark hair was twisted into a braid down her back. Teagan wore a skin-tight black tank top tucked into a pair of brown cargo pants that hugged her curves. A pair of sheaths hung from her belt on either hip. My guess was that she was some sort of badass shifter who could rip a vampire's throat out with her teeth.

I think I'm going to like this girl.

Teagan stepped forward and snatched the knife from

Fiona's outstretched hand. She ignored Fiona's question but kept her eyes on me.

"So, you're the girl Venn brought home?" Teagan asked as she slid her knife into its sheath.

I nodded. "The one and only."

"You heard all that?" Fiona asked, like it wasn't obvious. "Maybe you can do something to calm Ryland down later?"

Fiona made it sound like Teagan had some sort of power over Ryland. Maybe she wasn't a shifter but was a witch... or, like me, perhaps she was both.

My gaze traveled beyond Teagan. I took note of a queen-sized bed and two dressers side-by-side. The decor was simple and accented with neutral browns. That's when it clicked what kind of power she had over him, and it wasn't anything supernatural. Ryland was her boyfriend.

I need to get myself one of those.

The problem was, I had to actually leave the house if I wanted to meet anyone. I was never going to meet a guy while patrolling for vamps causing trouble.

"This is Rae, by the way," Fiona introduced. "She needs to borrow some clothes."

Teagan didn't say anything as Fiona crossed the room to her closet. Instead, she kept her attention on me. She stood so close that I could smell the scent of lavender on her clothes. She was two inches taller than me and stared down at me like I was supposed to be intimidated by her. I stared back with an equally intimidating glare.

"What are you?" Teagan asked curiously.

My brow furrowed. "Excuse me?"

Could she sense I was supernatural? She must've been a powerful witch.

"Venn wouldn't bring just anyone home," Teagan pointed out. "What kind of shifter are you?"

My eyes darted to Fiona across the room, but I only saw a glimpse of her backside in the walk-in closet. I didn't tell people I was a shifter. The only reason Venn knew was because he saw it. Even the witch who enchanted my clothes didn't know what I was. Luckily, she wasn't the kind of person who asked questions. She just took the money and did her thing.

I wasn't about to give up my secret to a girl I just met, no matter the fact that she could probably give me a run for my money in a fight.

I cleared my throat. "I'm a low witch. You?"

"Vampire slayer," Teagan said confidently, without missing a beat.

"Seriously?" I asked in disbelief.

Was she suggesting she was a supernatural "chosen one?" That didn't happen in real life, did it? Then again, eight years ago I would've said vampires, shifters, and witches didn't exist either.

"Don't let her fool you," Fiona said, emerging from the closet with an armful of clothes. "Teagan's entirely human."

"No way." The words slipped from my mouth before I could stop myself. Teagan seemed… tougher than that.

"What?" Teagan raised an eyebrow. "Humans aren't good enough for you?"

"No, I just—" I fumbled for the right words. *Crap.* "You really fight vampires?"

Teagan sucked her teeth. "On occasion."

"You *have* to have shifter blood in you," I insisted.

"Nope," Teagan said with certainty.

"How are you fast enough?" I asked.

"She doesn't need supernatural speed," Fiona said, like she was quoting Teagan's own words. She dropped her pile of clothes on the bed before turning to me. "All she needs is a clear shot of their heart."

"Yep," Teagan agreed proudly. "Stab them in the heart with anything, and they die."

I knew the drill. Vampires only dropped dead from a wound to the heart or brain, decapitation, or fire. They healed quickly from other injuries.

"You just have to get to them before they get to you," Teagan continued.

"*Stab first, ask questions later,*" Fiona said. "That's Tea's motto."

Teagan smirked. I liked her motto.

"Ryland would never let a vamp hurt her," Fiona said. "Anyway, Tea, are these pants fine to lend Rae?"

Teagan glanced at the cargo pants Fiona held up. "Not those."

Teagan marched across the room and scooped up the clothes on the bed and returned them to her closet. Fiona shot an apologetic look at me while we waited for Teagan to return.

"So..." I dragged out the word, partially to fill the silence. "Venn's a shifter, and Teagan's human. What are you?"

Oh, gosh. I hope that didn't sound rude.

Fiona sat on the bed. "Fox shifter."

Which meant Ryland was a shifter too.

"Is Sondra a shifter?" God, I was nosy. If she was Fiona's cousin, she could be anything depending on which side of the family Fiona inherited her shifter magic from. "When do I get to meet her? I want to tell her how much I love her drawings."

Teagan exited the closet while I spoke. She froze in place and exchanged a wary glance with Fiona.

Fiona was the one to answer. "Sondra's... not here right now. But if everything goes well, you should be able to meet her soon."

I didn't have a chance to ask where Sondra was or when she'd return as Teagan shoved a pile of neatly folded clothes in my direction.

"Here," she said. "These should fit. You can change in the bathroom. It's the next door on the right down the hall."

I took the pile of clothes in my hands. "Thanks."

Teagan grabbed a jacket off her dresser and slipped it on. It fell to the top of her thighs and covered up the knives on her hips.

Fiona stood. "Let me know when you're done so we can throw your pants in the wash."

I shot back a smile. It was nice of her to offer. It'd save me a few quarters and a night at the laundromat.

I turned and stepped out into the hall just in time to see Venn climbing the stairs. A smile spread across his face when he spotted me. My breath stalled in my chest, and my knees went weak under his stare. What the frick? My insides were rock-solid. They shouldn't be turning to mush, especially not for a guy I just barely met.

Venn reached the top of the steps and stopped with one hand on the banister. "You almost ready?"

"Yeah, I..." I didn't know what to say. My eyes dropped to the clothes in my hands. "I just have to change. I'll be out in a minute."

"Try not to be too long," Venn suggested. "Ryland wants to get going soon."

I was about to turn to the bathroom but paused. "Hey, Venn."

"Yeah?" he asked softly, his eyes still fixed on me.

I wasn't sure why I stopped or what I was going to say. All I knew was that I didn't want to step out of the room without him.

Stop acting weird!

"Thank you," I finally said while fidgeting with a loose thread on the tank top I held. "I mean, Ryland was right. You don't have a reason to trust me. So I just wanted to say thanks for offering to help."

Venn stepped forward and reached out like he was about to touch me, but he pulled away at the last second. I had the unnatural urge to accept his invitation and close the distance between us.

"It's no problem," he said.

An awkward silence followed, and I contemplated saying more. Several seconds passed, but nothing came out of my mouth. It felt too late to break the silence now, so I turned to the bathroom without another word.

Inside the bathroom, I forced Venn from my mind, and my thoughts turned to Cowen. My heart pounded as I rushed to slip into Teagan's clothes. In a matter of minutes, I'd be back on my way to tracking down the Soulless.

Watch out, Fangs. Here I come.

<hr>

When Ryland said we were going after Cowen, I thought we were headed to kick some vampire ass. As in, I thought Ryland knew where to find him. Turns out he didn't have a clue.

We pulled up in front of the bar I cornered Cowen outside of last night. The sign above the door read *Red Whiskey*. This was a hot hangout for vamps since they sold alcohol *and* blood—fresh from the blood banks, thank God—but we wouldn't find a vamp hanging out here in the middle of the day.

"I thought you knew how to track this guy down," I accused Venn when he parked the car.

Venn turned in his seat to explain. "This is as far as we tracked him. We got a tip that this is his favorite hangout spot, but now that he knows we can find him here, we're not sure he'll be back. We're here to figure out where to find him next."

"Unfortunately," Ryland cut in, "Venn acted on pure emotion last night without calling in the rest of us, so I'll be doing the talking this time."

"Or maybe *I* should," Teagan offered from next to me in the back seat.

"No," Ryland stated sternly.

"You scare people away," Teagan accused.

"If you don't want to scare people, send me in," Fiona argued. With her small frame and sweet smile, she didn't look like she was capable of hurting a fly. She was right that no one would be intimidated by her.

Before the group could come to an agreement, Venn opened his door and stepped out of the car. Ryland fumbled with his door handle and kicked the passenger-side door open. I draped my purse strap over my shoulder and scrambled out of the car behind them. Teagan and Fiona followed closely behind.

Ryland's long legs carried him ahead of Venn so that he was the first to reach the door. He gripped the handle so hard that I was surprised it didn't crush beneath his grip like a soda can.

The building had no windows, and the lights were dim when we entered. A long bar lined with stools ran the length of the building to our right, while other tables filled the rest of the space. The chairs were all empty, and the building was silent apart from the sound of an air conditioner whirring. The back of the bar housed a lounge and a pool table. The distinct smell of floor cleaner filled my nostrils, masking any other scents that may have permeated into the walls and furniture.

Before any of us had a chance to speak, a man emerged from a door behind the bar. He held a drying towel in his hands and had a bored expression fixed to his face. He was attractive and looked to be in his late twenties or early thirties. For a vamp-friendly bar, I expected to find vampires running the place, but this guy's eyes were blue—not a hint of silver present.

Probably a blood slave, I thought. I hated that I couldn't tell what he was. Someday, I was going to figure out how to identify the difference between witches, shifters, and humans.

Fiona's eyes traveled the length of his body. It took everything I had to hold in my laughter. He was at least a decade older than her, and she was totally checking him out.

"Sorry, folks," he said in a smooth voice. I noticed the name on his uniform read *Alex*. "We're closed."

"The door was unlocked," Ryland responded, as if that was an excuse for the guy to serve us a drink—not that any of us were even of legal age. A lot had changed in the past eight years, but the drinking age was still twenty-one.

"Our hours are posted out front," Alex informed us, like leaving the door unlocked during off-hours was a common occurrence. "If you want to avoid the vamp crowd, it's best to come early."

Ryland stepped forward until he was right next to the bar. "Thanks for the tip, but actually, we're not here for a drink. We're looking for someone who frequents this establishment."

'Frequents this establishment?' He sounds so formal when he wants to.

"Can you help us?" Ryland asked.

Alex tossed the towel over his shoulder and leaned against the counter behind the bar, looking amused. "Who are you looking for?"

"His name's Cowen," Ryland answered.

Alex pressed his lips together. "He's a vamp? Brown hair, scar on his wrist?"

So Alex knows Cowen's a Soulless. Am I the only one who didn't know there was a Soulless running around Nocton?

Ryland nodded.

"Yeah, he's a regular, but I don't know where to find him," Alex said.

Too bad. I was really looking forward to beating information out of someone. Except Alex didn't look like he deserved a beating, and I didn't pick a fight without a reason.

Alex cocked his head in the direction of the kitchen and raised his voice. "Hey, Kieren. Come here a minute."

A huge guy that took up the entire doorway stepped into the room. Ryland's arms were like twigs compared to this guy. It didn't matter that I didn't have the sense to spot supernatural beings; I was totally pegging this guy as a shifter.

"They're looking for Cowen," Alex explained.

Kieren crossed his massive arms, and his eyes traveled over the group; first to Fiona, then to me. I shifted uncomfortably, like I'd just been violated by a simple glance. Maybe *this* guy deserved a punch to the groin. His gaze skipped straight over Venn and landed on Teagan. She didn't even blink.

"I might know Cowen," Kieren said in a deep voice.

"Well enough to know where to find him?" Ryland asked.

"That depends..." Kieren dragged out.

"On?" Ryland pressed.

Kieren smirked. "On how valuable the information is to you."

I glanced to Venn to see his jaw was tense. His eyes met mine, but I couldn't read his expression.

Ryland sighed, like he was hoping it wouldn't come to this. "What's your price?"

Kieren still hadn't taken his eyes off Teagan. She held his gaze without a single sign of fear. It was like she was used to guys looking at her like that—like a piece of meat. I think I felt uncomfortable enough for the both of us.

"What are you willing to pay?" Kieren asked with a raised eyebrow.

Ryland dug into his back pocket for his wallet and slapped a pile of bills on the bar. "Look, we don't have a lot of money, but we really need to find this guy. Can you help us or not?"

Kieren glanced down at the money but didn't move to take it. Beside him, Alex looked like he was itching to snatch it up.

"I can help," Kieren stated flatly, "but I don't want your money."

"What *do* you want?" Ryland asked.

Kieren didn't even hesitate. He cocked his head toward Teagan. "I'll take the girl."

Disgust hit my stomach at the suggestion. Fiona gasped,

and Venn's expression hardened. Teagan just rolled her eyes, as if it was all too predictable.

"No," Ryland declined immediately.

Kieren stepped forward and placed his palms flat on the bar. Though there was a countertop between them, Ryland took a step back to distance himself from Kieren. A tingle spread across my skin in preparation to shift.

Cool down, I told myself. Even though I had a rule about shifting in front of people, I *would* shift if it came to that.

"Maybe let the girl decide for herself," Kieren suggested.

Ooh, what a gentleman...

Teagan's expression remained static. Clearly, this guy didn't scare her. Finally, she turned to Ryland. "Let's go. We'll find Cowen another way."

Teagan started for the door, but Kieren's voice stopped her.

"Come on," he said. "I'm only asking for one night."

Teagan whirled around. "And I'm saying *no.*"

"Fine," Kieren said with a shrug, like it didn't really matter to him either way. "But I know where to find him. If you leave, you might never know."

"Stop pushing it!" Ryland snapped. He leaned over the bar until his nose was only inches from Kieren's. "She said no."

I held my breath as the two stared each other down. I half expected one of them to spontaneously combust under the other's narrowed gaze.

Teagan stepped to Ryland's side, breaking the staring contest between the two guys. "Name us another price."

Kieren straightened. "I gave you my price. Take it or leave it."

Teagan gritted her teeth. "We'll leave it. Have a nice day."

Teagan's hand slapped to the counter to grab the wad of cash Ryland had placed there. In a flash, Kieren's arm shot out to grab Teagan's wrist.

And that's when Ryland lost it.

5

Chaos broke out all within a single second.

One moment, Ryland was looking up at Kieren with a narrowed, challenging gaze, and the next, his legs lengthened so that he towered above Kieren. Ryland's arms thickened, and brown fur sprouted all across his body.

Kieren dropped Teagan's hand and jumped back. His body shortened and morphed into a black creature not much bigger than I was.

At the same time, Venn whirled around and spread his arms out, catching me and Fiona at the same time. I stumbled backward into the table behind us, and the edge of it slammed into my backbone. Fiona fell over one of the chairs and crashed to the ground.

I suffered only a moment of disorientation, but when my attention turned back to the rest of the room, Ryland and Kieren had already fully shifted. Teagan had her knives out in under a second, looking determined to use them if she had to.

A terrifying roar filled the room, sending a surge of adrenaline through my veins. Ryland had grown to three times his normal size, so big that four stools and a table had been knocked out of the way in his transformation. He bared his large, pointed canines as a deep roar erupted from his chest.

A bear. Ryland's a freaking bear shifter.

That explained the tree trunk arms he had.

In front of him, a large cat with a black coat stood atop the bar, its lips curled back over its teeth. The t-shirt Kieren had been wearing hung from the jaguar's body.

That tingle of shifter magic returned and traveled all the way up my spine. I was a split second away from shifting, ready to peck some eyes out if necessary. I stood farthest from the bar in human form, bracing myself. Venn and Fiona stepped forward, Venn in his wolf form and Fiona in her fox form. Alex raced through the door to the kitchen, running away from the fight.

Another beat passed as Ryland and Kieren bared their equally terrifying teeth at each other. Then, without warning, Kieren lunged.

It all happened in a blur. One second, Kieren was standing atop the bar in his jaguar form eye-to-eye with Ryland's bear. The next, he was on top of him, clawing into the flesh on his neck. Teagan lunged forward, swiping one of her knives at Kieren. She just barely caught him in the back leg.

Ryland spun around. His head jerked from side to side as he tried to throw Kieren off of him. His body slammed into Teagan, knocking her off balance and sending her crashing into a nearby table. Ryland didn't even notice.

I rushed across the room to Teagan and helped her to her feet. She shrugged me off but followed me in haste around the bar. Venn's howls filled the air, as if he was trying to talk some sense into Ryland in his shifted form.

Ryland went wild trying to buck Kieren off of him, but

Kieren's claws dug into Ryland's back. Table and chairs screeched across the floor as Ryland slammed into them. Beside me, Teagan popped her head up over the bar and pulled an arm back, a knife ready between her fingers.

I caught her wrist before she could throw it. "Don't," I hissed. "You could hit Ryland."

Teagan didn't have a moment to respond. A split second later, Kieren's teeth sunk into the back of Ryland's neck, and Ryland shot to his hind legs. If I hadn't stopped Teagan, there was a good chance Ryland would have a knife sticking out of his back right now.

Ryland fell sideways. The nearest table crumbled beneath his weight, and the two shifters crashed to the ground. Ryland twisted his massive head, and his powerful jaws snapped at Kieren, who still hadn't loosened his grip.

This was *way* out of hand.

I didn't think. I just *acted*. In a mere second, my five-foot-four-frame shrank. The clothes I'd been wearing dropped around me in a heap. I flapped my wings and shot across the room until I was in Kieren's face, clawing at any flesh I could find and blocking his vision with my wings.

While I had him momentarily distracted, Venn jumped forward. His weight slammed into Kieren, knocking him several feet away from Ryland. A high-pitched whimper filled the air. Ryland regained his footing, but Kieren collapsed under his front paw when he tried to right himself. Venn stood between the two, growling at Kieren.

Finally, Kieren dropped his gaze in surrender, and Venn's growl died down. Ryland shifted back into human form and wiped the blood from the puncture wounds left by Kieren's teeth.

I landed behind the bar and shifted. Teagan's eyes went wide. Fiona rushed around the side of the bar while I was pulling my shirt back on. Luckily, I'd kept my enchanted underwear on from earlier, so I didn't have to flash anyone. Good thing, too, because Teagan's wide eyes were still on me. I would've felt a hundred times more uncomfortable if my tits were hanging out.

"Are you two okay?" Fiona asked in a rush, kneeling down beside us.

Teagan ignored her. "Why didn't you tell us you were a shifter?"

I stood to pull my pants back on. "I didn't realize I was obligated to."

"A *raven?*" Teagan hissed.

I ignored her. I snatched up my bag and hopped over the top of the bar. By now, Venn and Kieren were back in human form, but Kieren was still on the ground. He wore nothing but his ripped t-shirt, leaving all his goods hanging out in the open. He didn't even seem to notice as he clutched his left hand with his right.

"You broke my hand!" Kieren roared at Venn before proceeding to call him a slew of horrible names.

"Yeah, well, you deserved it!" Venn snapped back.

Kieren sucked in deep breaths as he got to his knees. "Leave! All of you!"

Ryland didn't waste a second. He took Teagan's hand and started for the door.

"Alex!" Kieren called on his way to the kitchen. "Lock the doors and get the car. We're going to the hospital."

Ha! The hospital. Too bad he didn't know a good witch. Though, healing spells could be just as costly as hospital bills, but at least he wouldn't have to suffer through the pain. Which, judging by this guy's use of colorful words, could really brighten his day.

"Wait!" I blurted before I could stop myself.

Everyone froze to look at me.

Oh, crap. I couldn't go through with what I was just about to say. Sure, I could heal myself from time to time, but I'd never healed someone else before. He could end up with boils across his skin or something gross like that. There was a reason I didn't conjure magic for profit.

But... the chance to find Cowen—to find my sister—was *far* more valuable than any monetary payment. Could it really hurt to *try*?

Yes, I told myself. Everyone was eyeing me, waiting for me to explain my sudden outburst.

I can't believe I'm doing this, I thought, my hands shaking.

I cleared my throat. "I'll help you."

"Help me?" Kieren asked skeptically. He was behind the bar now, struggling to pull on his pants with one hand—thank God, because I didn't think I'd be able to look him in the eye otherwise.

"I'm a witch," I explained. "I'll heal your hand. It will save you a trip to the hospital, emergency room bills, and weeks of recovery."

Kieren hesitated. "You'll do all that *if* I tell you where to find Cowen?"

"Yes," I replied.

Kieren scoffed. "Screw you."

"Seriously?" I snapped as he turned away. "The information is *that* valuable to you?"

"No," Kieren barked, spinning back toward me. "But

pissing you people off is pretty damn satisfying. Now get out of my bar."

"Come on," Venn said to me in a low voice, encouraging me to follow him. "You don't have to do this."

Kieren cursed under his breath.

"I can make the pain go away," I stated confidently. The truth was, I had no idea if my healing spell would work on someone else. But it wasn't like I was above conning a guy who clearly had worse morals than I did.

Kieren grimaced, like he was fighting an internal battle on whether or not to save his hand or save his pride.

"All you have to do is tell us where to find Cowen," I pressed.

Kieren's jaw remained tense. "So you break my hand to use it as a trade for information? You should be fixing it without asking anything in return."

"Hey," I said like it didn't matter to me one way or the other. I was totally bluffing; I really wanted the information. "I'm not the one who broke your hand. If you don't want to take my offer, you're free to go to the hospital on your own."

A long pause passed through the bar. My shoulders tensed with each passing second.

Finally, Kieren spoke. "Fine."

Yes!

"First you give us what we want," I demanded.

"No way," Kieren protested. "You'll just walk out of here without helping me."

"I won't," I swore. But I needed him to fulfill his side of the bargain first in case my spell didn't work.

"How do I know you're not lying to me?" Kieren asked.

Good question.

I held my head high. "I guess we're just going to have to trust each other."

Kieren didn't look like he trusted me one bit, but he *did* look desperate.

"Okay," he reluctantly agreed. "Cowen lives with a group of vampires on the corner of Cramer and Valander. It's the big white house with red shutters. Now will you fix my effing hand?"

A sense of victory washed over me. *One step closer.*

My excitement didn't last long. If this spell didn't go well, I'd better be ready to run.

"Sit," I instructed Kieren, pulling out one of the stools next to the bar.

Kieren glared at the group of shifters—and one human—behind me, but he rounded the bar and sat anyway. I took one glance at Venn and his family to see they all had a look of intrigue in their eyes. They were probably just as curious as I was to see how this was going to pan out.

I ignored their stares and pulled a second stool up beside Kieren. I grabbed my spell book from my bag and flipped it open to the spell I'd used last night. My eyes scanned the incantation. I should've had it memorized by now, but I had a terrible memory when it came to spells. That was probably one of the reasons I was such a bad spellcaster.

"Are we gonna do this or what?" Kieren asked through clenched teeth. "Because this hurts like a mother—"

"Yes," I replied quickly. "Give me your hand."

Kieren's bruised hand hung limp as he extended his arm toward me. Gently, I took his wounded hand in mine. He didn't show any emotion, like he was too tough for that.

Seconds ticked by, but I couldn't bring myself to mutter the incantation.

"Let's get this over already," Kieren mumbled.

Right. Okay, Rachel, just say the incantation, then you can get out of here.

I began reading the spell from my book, focusing only on the words and Kieren's hand in mine. I neared the end of the incantation, but Kieren's face remained expressionless. I couldn't tell if he was still in pain or not.

Here come the boils.

Just as I thought it, a sharp, stabbing pain shot through my left hand. It hurt so bad that I sprang up from my chair and let out a high-pitched squeal. Kieren's face lit up with alarm, but by the time he spoke, the pain in my hand was already gone.

"What happened?" he demanded.

I didn't have an answer. I'd never experienced something like that before. Had my spell backfired? Could it do that?

"It didn't work!" Kieren roared.

"It—it didn't?" God, I sounded like I had no idea what I was doing. Which, to be fair, I didn't. Not really.

"No, it didn't!" Kieren cried, shooting up from his stool. He looked like he was two seconds away from going all maniac-jaguar on us again. "I gave you the information you asked for. You owe me a good hand!"

Venn rushed forward before Kieren got mad enough to punch me out with his good hand. "Let her try again. Some-times it takes a few tries."

Kieren paused, but he didn't look convinced.

"I saw her perform a healing spell last night," Venn said in an attempt to calm Kieren down.

Just tell the whole world, why don't you, Venn? Everyone's going to want me to heal them. The joke's on them, since I can't cast a decent spell to save my life.

"She can do it," Venn said. "Let her give it another shot."

Okay, maybe I could cast a spell to save *my* life, but I wasn't sure I could cast a spell to save someone else's.

Kieren slumped back into his stool. "Fine, but if this doesn't work…"

I was incredibly grateful that he didn't finish that sentence.

Venn stood behind me and squeezed my shoulders. Warm tingles spread down my arms, calming me. It was almost as if he had magic of his own, though I figured he would've told me by now if he was a witch. My shoulders relaxed beneath the weight of his comforting hands.

"You can do this," Venn whispered in my ear. "You cast the same spell last night, and it worked. You can do it again. I know you have it in you. You just have to believe in yourself."

I took a deep breath. *He's right. I can do this.*

Taking Kieren's hand in mine again, I reread the incantation. This *had* to work.

"It's not working," Kieren said, disgruntled.

Or not…

"Remember why you're doing this," Venn whispered from beside me.

I'm doing this to find Cowen, I told myself. *Because without him, I'll never find Jenna. I'm doing this for my sister.*

I read through the incantation a third time. All my thoughts turned to Jenna. I pictured her soft blue eyes and long brown hair. In my mind, she hadn't aged a day since I last saw her. She was still eighteen and drop-dead gorgeous, with long lashes and a dimple on the right side of her face. I imagined the smile that would spread across her face when I found her. I pictured her pulling me into a tight hug. She'd squeeze me until I couldn't breathe, like she used to do when we were kids.

I missed you so much, rugrat! Jenna would say.

I would cry, even though I'd try not to. *I missed you, too, Jenna-Bean.*

Before I realized it, I'd already reached the end of the incantation. Kieren continued to stare at me in skepticism.

"Better?" I asked. I couldn't read him.

"Better," Kieren said bitterly, "but not fixed."

I could hardly believe my ears.

"Then it worked," I told him, standing and scooping up my spell book. "The pain will start to go away slowly, and it should be completely healed within a couple of days."

Kieren didn't look happy, but he couldn't deny that I'd held up my end of the bargain. Which I still couldn't believe.

"Thank you for your cooperation," I said before turning to leave.

Kieren scoffed, like he didn't think of it as cooperation in the slightest.

Venn, Ryland, Teagan, and Fiona all headed to the door with me, no doubt as eager as I was to escape this place as quickly as possible.

"I don't want to see any of you back here!" Kieren called before we stepped outside. "You hear me?"

Obviously, I was never going back there. He'd probably demand we pay for the broken tables, and I certainly didn't have that kind of cash lying around.

Outside, Fiona rammed into me, pulling me into a tight hug.

"*Ohf.*" A breath of air escaped my lungs.

"Thank you *so* much!" Fiona continued to squeeze me.

"For what?" I asked on our way to the car. "All I did was heal the guy's hand."

And I probably didn't do a very good job of it, I told myself.

"You did more than that, though," Venn insisted, pulling out his keys. "You got him to tell us where to find Cowen."

"Yeah," Fiona agreed. "Teagan wasn't any help."

Teagan slugged Fiona as she ducked into the car.

"Ow!" Fiona complained, holding on to her shoulder.

"You seriously expected me to sleep with that guy?" Teagan asked in disbelief.

"No," Ryland said firmly as he slid into the passenger seat. "None of us would've let you do something like that."

Teagan's expression softened, but it only lasted a second before she turned to me with a raised eyebrow. "I thought you said you were a low witch."

I shrugged. "Mostly. I guess I just have a gift for healing."

"And a bit of shifter magic," Fiona pointed out, gazing at me in admiration. "You're the Ravenite, aren't you?"

I sighed. There was no point in denying it. There weren't exactly hundreds of raven shifters running around Nocton.

"I do what's necessary," I said, adding a hint of warning to my tone. "So… are we gonna go get this vamp or what?"

Venn pulled out onto the street.

"Believe me," Ryland said. "I wanna go after him as soon as possible, too, but you heard what Kieren said. Cowen lives with a bunch of other vamps. We have to be careful. There's a good chance they outnumber us."

"So, what do we do?" Fiona asked, hopeless.

Ryland paused a beat and glanced to the sky. The sun was hidden behind a thick layer of clouds, so it wasn't going to help us much today. Sure, it would slow the vampires down and maybe give them a few blisters, but it wasn't enough to make them retreat like it would if the sun were out.

"We wait until nightfall," he decided. "It'll give us enough time to scope out the place. Plus, most of the vamps will leave by then, so we can crash the nest while there are fewer to deal with. Maybe Cowen will make an appearance himself."

"I say we bust down the place right now," Teagan voted. "We don't have the time to waste."

"Yeah, well, I'm not gonna walk straight into a full vampire nest and lose any one of you," Ryland replied with a harsh tone. He had a point.

"In that case," Teagan agreed, "I'm going to need more knives."

6

———

Night fell, and darkness enveloped the city, but the minutes on Venn's dashboard continued to tick by, and still no sign of Cowen. We'd been sitting in the car a few doors down from the white house on the corner for hours, and we had yet to see a single person come or go.

"Maybe Kieren lied," Fiona theorized, pausing momentarily from blowing air across the back of Teagan's neck. She'd been doing it for the last several minutes to try to get a reaction out of her. Either Teagan hadn't noticed or she was purposely ignoring Fiona. I'd been trying to hold in a laugh because it seemed like something my sister would do when she was bored.

Venn shook his head. "I don't think he lied. I mean, the house is here like he said."

There was no arguing that, considering it was probably the only white house with red shutters in town. The house was old, with various peaks in the roof, two chimneys, and peeling paint siding. Crooked wooden stairs led up to a front porch that looked like it creaked with every step. The house rose two stories high and looked big enough to have at least five bedrooms on the top floor. It certainly *looked* like something a vamp would live in, with the whole haunted-house vibe it had going on.

"If he didn't lie, then where's Cowen?" Ryland asked with a tense jaw, as if Venn was supposed to know the answer.

"Calm down, love," Teagan said in a soothing voice.

She reached forward from the back seat to run her hand across Ryland's shoulder. He breathed a sigh and laced his fingers through hers, pulling her hand to his lips and brushing a kiss across it.

Damn, they were so cute together. I needed to get myself someone like Teagan, a partner who could calm me with a single touch.

Teagan jumped in her seat and swatted at Fiona. "Would you stop it?!" she snapped.

Or, you know, I could just get myself the type of person who would bite my hand off just for kicks.

"Are you being annoying again, Fiona?" Ryland scolded.

Fiona rolled her eyes. "*Again?* You mean *still?*"

Ryland didn't even justify her answer with a response. Fiona frowned and folded her hands in her lap. Clearly, sitting still was getting to her.

"Maybe we missed the vamps," I suggested. "They could be leaving through the back door."

Ryland let out a groan, like he couldn't believe he hadn't thought of it before.

Yeah, we were officially idiots.

Ryland kicked his door open before anyone could get in another word. "You wanna come stake it out with me, Tea?"

A wide smile spread across her face, like she was hoping they'd run into trouble at the back of the house.

"I'm coming, too!" Fiona volunteered, rushing out of the car behind Teagan.

An uncomfortable silence filled the air when the doors shut behind them, leaving Venn and me alone in the car. The only sound came from Venn reaching into the glove compartment followed by the rustle of a plastic bag. Judging by the scent that hit me from the back seat, I guessed he was snacking on cheesy snack mix. My favorite, too, and the greedy bastard didn't even offer to share.

A full minute must've passed without either of us saying a word, but it felt more like an hour. I wanted to say something, but I couldn't come up with anything that wouldn't make me sound like an idiot.

"You can come sit up here," Venn offered.

"Oh, thank God," I blurted, grateful that someone finally broke the silence. I wanted to shove the words back in my mouth as soon as I said them.

"God has nothing to do with it," Venn joked as I climbed over the middle console and settled into the front seat.

"He doesn't?" I teased back.

Good thing, too, since I didn't believe in God. Somehow, I didn't think vampires and shifters fit into the God story, though some people claimed that vampires were just demons who'd escaped from Hell and had come to possess their loved ones. It might've been believable except for the fact that crucifixes and holy water didn't work on them. If I had a nickel for every time I rolled my eyes at the demon theory, I'd be able to afford a *far* better apartment.

"So, you don't think vampires are spawns of Satan?" I asked, mostly to keep the silence from once again entering the car.

Venn smirked and let out a light laugh. "No, I don't."

I leaned toward him with curiosity in my eyes. The scent of the snack mix in his lap filled my nose. My pulse quickened with each inch I came closer to him, but I ignored it. "Then where'd they come from?"

"Well, I won't claim to know *everything*," he admitted, holding out his bag toward me.

Score!

"But what I do know makes a lot of sense," he said.

"Oh?" I raised my eyebrows and plunged my hand into the bag. "What is it that you know?"

Venn smirked, looking positively proud of himself. "For starters, I know how magic works."

I scoffed and tossed a handful of cheesy crackers into my mouth. "No, you don't."

Even Devin, my boss, didn't truly know how magic worked, though that shouldn't have surprised me. It was clear he was only in the business for the money.

Venn returned the bag to his lap. "You've never hung out with a high witch before, have you?"

"I paid a high witch to enchant my clothes, if that counts," I told him.

Venn shook his head. "Doesn't count. Not unless she told you how she did it."

"She didn't," I said with a full mouth.

I must look like such a lady.

Venn popped another handful of snack mix into his mouth then wiped his hand on his jeans. "Ever heard of Synchrony?"

I furrowed my brow, not sure what he meant. "I've heard the word before."

"But do you know what it means?" he asked.

"Um… are you asking me to recite the definition from the dictionary?" I replied, insulted.

Venn laughed. "No. I'm talking in a philosophical sense. Synchrony is the force that creates and sustains life. It's responsible for the balance within the universe."

"Okay…" I dragged out the word. "I'm intrigued."

Though it's probably just nonsense.

"Essentially, Synchrony is God but without conscious thought," Venn explained. "It's more closely related to nature. It's just something that *is*, like electricity."

"Really?" I asked skeptically. He expected me to believe this? I didn't know what to believe these days, but I wasn't buying that.

"I can't explain it like Sondra can," Venn said, "but basically, she says that Synchrony is the life-sustaining force that's been around since the Big Bang."

"You're saying magic has been around forever?" I asked. Some theories claimed magic was always there. Others said it came here from another world when Valkas showed up—and that he was from that other world, too. I still didn't know which theory to go with.

"Yes," Venn answered. "Magic has always existed in our world. It just wasn't made public until eight years ago. Before that, the secrets of Synchrony were kept within the supernatural community. It was the only way people escaped persecution."

"So in your story, magic and Synchrony are the same thing?" I asked.

"Not exactly," Venn said. "That's like asking if light and electricity are the same thing. Magic is what happens when you access Synchrony, but Synchrony itself is bigger than that. It's what creates life—creates souls—and what drives fate."

"Fate?" I laughed. Venn was officially a nutcase… A nutcase

who made butterflies dance around in my stomach. I mentally squashed the suckers.

"Yes," Venn stated flatly.

My laughter instantly died. Woops. I was being a total ass.

My voice softened. "I'm sorry. I'm listening. Tell me more."

Venn eyed me, like he couldn't tell if he should keep going or not. I really did feel bad about laughing at him.

Finally, he continued. "I believe there are no coincidences in life; only balance. We have an equal give and take relationship with Synchrony. If you bring positivity into the world, Synchrony will deliver more positive things into your life. Accessing the Synchrony force—or doing magic—has consequences because it all balances out."

"Okay," I said, trying to keep an open mind. "But not all magic *does* have consequences."

"Not all consequences are negative," Venn said. "But Synchrony always reacts. *How* it reacts depends on your intentions when you cast a spell. If you cast the spell with positive intentions, you will get positive results. The bigger the spell, the more consequences, like how trying to bring someone back to life could trap their soul in their body. Well-intentioned spells won't have bad consequences. That's probably why you're so good at healing. On the other hand, dark magic almost always results in negative outcomes because there are very few dark spells that can be cast with pure intentions."

"Why would anyone practice dark magic, then?" I asked.

Ha! Plot hole!

Venn frowned. "Because they honestly believe they're in the right."

I narrowed my eyes in thought, trying to absorb everything he was saying.

"Synchrony reflects your intentions back on you," Venn continued. "You can never cast a perfect spell if you're doing it for selfish reasons or if you're trying to hurt someone else."

"That doesn't make any sense," I argued. I don't know why I didn't want to believe Venn. Maybe I didn't want to believe there were people out there with the answer and I'd gone so long without knowing it. "I tried to heal Kieren earlier, and the spell backfired on me. I wasn't being selfish or trying to hurt him."

"Maybe not," Venn agreed with a shrug, "but you were still projecting negative energy."

"No, I wasn't," I insisted. He couldn't even *do* magic, but he was going to sit here and tell me all about how I'd been doing it wrong?

Jerk.

Venn didn't seem to notice my furrowed brow. "The thing about Synchrony is that it doesn't recognize good versus evil. Instead, it recognizes positive energy versus negative energy. Your beliefs and intentions affect how Synchrony responds."

"How so?" I asked. He wasn't suggesting I was carrying around negative energy like some sort of evil witch, was he?

"You have to believe in your ability and the reasons for why you're casting the spell." Venn looked at me with a pointed expression, like he was accusing me of something. I just wasn't sure what he was accusing me of. "A witch who doubts herself is much more susceptible to consequences."

"I do not doubt myself!" I defended.

"Yes, you do," Venn said, like it was fact.

Any lingering butterflies in my stomach were now officially dead.

"You don't know anything about me," I replied in disgust.

Venn shrugged. "You're right, I don't. But I know how

Synchrony works, and I know you're a lot more powerful than you give yourself credit for."

Ugh, here comes the flattery, like he wasn't just insulting me a moment ago.

"I know what I'm capable of," I stated.

Venn peeled his gaze off me and looked back toward the house. "Do you? Because you said you've never worked with a high witch before. You might learn a lot by having a mentor."

"Yes," I agreed sarcastically, "because high witches willing to mentor me on my budget drop out of the sky every day. How do you know all this anyway?"

Venn blinked several times before answering. "Because Sondra's a high witch. She told me."

My blood stopped in my veins. Mind. Officially. Blown.

These people were living with a high witch, and this just happened to be the first time anyone mentioned it to me? High witches were rare, and most of them were living in luxury, not still hanging around in a city like Nocton.

"Seriously?" My tone came out softer this time, all the offense removed from my voice. "Could she teach me?"

For free, obviously, because Devin barely pays me minimum wage.

"I can't speak for her," Venn said, "but I'm sure she'd be happy to teach you a thing or two once we get her back."

I nearly choked on the handful of snack mix I'd just shoved in my mouth. "Get her back? Where is she?"

Venn swallowed hard, like he was contemplating whether or not to trust me with the truth. "She was… taken."

"Oh, my God!" I cried. "Like, kidnapped?"

Venn nodded somberly. "Yes. She's being held for ransom. That's why we're after Cowen. He stole the thing we need to get her back."

I was just about to ask what it was he needed when Venn's entire body stiffened, halting my words in their tracks. I followed his gaze to see a male figure emerging from the house we'd been watching.

This jackhole is officially going down.

Before I could suggest calling Ryland and telling him we spotted movement, Venn's car door slammed behind him. Outside the car, Venn lunged forward, shifting into wolf form mid-air.

He raced after Cowen.

7

I kicked my door open and sprinted behind Venn. In his shifted form, Venn was *fast*. The black wolf slammed into the vampire and knocked him to the sidewalk before I was even halfway across the street. Venn's head snapped to the side as the vampire's fist connected with his jaw. It didn't even seem to faze Venn.

Venn's jaw snapped at the vamp in warning, and his paws pressed down on his chest. The vamp stopped struggling to hiss in Venn's face just as I reached them. Every muscle in Venn's body froze—like time altogether had stopped.

The light from the nearest street lamp caught the vampire's face. I, too, stopped in my tracks. The man stared back at Venn with hauntingly silver eyes. Fangs protruded from his mouth, but the shape of his jaw was unfamiliar. His hair was slicked back, like he was trying to channel an old-school Dracula vibe. Though he had similar hair color and an almost identical build to Cowen, we had the wrong guy.

Dracula's head swung forward in a flash, knocking into

Venn's snout with a sickening *thud*. Venn reeled backward on instinct. Dracula rolled in the grass, freeing himself from Venn's grasp. He dodged around Venn's outstretched paws and made a run for it, but he must've not seen me there, because he headed straight in my direction.

I didn't have time to think about what to do next. All I knew was that I wasn't ready to let this guy go without asking him some questions. I sprang from the pavement and leapt forward, catching the vampire around the middle and tackling him to the ground.

He quickly freed himself and scurried to his feet. Before he could make it far, Venn was on the other side of him, blocking his path. Dracula whirled around, but I skirted in front of him, ready to kick him in the royal jewels if it came to that. He hesitated, his nostrils flaring. His eyes dropped to my neck with a hungry look in then.

Oh, hell no. He looked like he had every intention of ripping out my jugular and using it as a straw.

"We're not here to hurt you," I said in a rush, hoping we could work this out civilly.

Dracula held his hands up in surrender, but I suspected he only stopped because I'd piqued his interest. My eyes darted to his wrists, just in case, but the skin on his arms was smooth.

"Then why'd your boyfriend try to knock me out?" he asked begrudgingly.

Boyfriend?

Venn stood on his hind legs, and the fur disappeared from his body as he shifted. He wiped the blood from his lip but barely stole a glance at it, like it didn't really matter.

"We thought you were someone else," Venn said without regret. "If he'd seen me first, he would've run."

Strike first. Ask questions later. I like Venn's style.

"Obviously, you have the wrong guy," Dracula snapped, glancing between the two of us.

"Is Cowen around?" I asked—or rather, demanded.

The vamp narrowed his gaze, but his eyes continued to flicker down to my throat. "Cowen? He hasn't lived here in years."

Venn cursed under his breath, and I was sure the blood had drained from my face.

"Years?" The word passed by my lips breathlessly.

"You deaf?" Dracula mocked. He inched away from us like we wouldn't notice.

"No," I answered, "but I'm a shifter who's strong as hell, so I suggest you refrain from the insults."

The vamp stopped retreating. "What do you want?"

"We want to know where to find Cowen," Venn answered. "That's all."

"I don't know where to find him." Dracula sounded like he was telling the truth. But then again, he *was* a vampire, and I had yet to meet a vamp who wasn't completely heartless.

"Are you sure?" I asked, using my most threatening voice.

I liked to think I sounded terrifying, but I must've not looked the part, because he didn't seem particularly scared of me. When his eyes darted to Venn, though, he sure looked wary.

"I hardly knew the guy," Dracula admitted, still looking at me like he'd enjoy me for his next meal. "He was just a roommate. He left a few months after I moved in."

"Were any of your other roommates close to him?" Venn asked.

The vamp rolled his eyes and turned to the car beside us

on the curb to climb inside. "I'm not some messenger boy. If you want to know more about him—"

I grabbed his door before he could slam it. He sat in the driver's seat, trying to wrench it out of my grasp, but I had a firm hold on it. The vamp looked up at me in shock, like he thought I'd been bluffing when I said I was strong.

"My *boyfriend* asked you a question," I stated in my most intimidating voice. "I suggest you answer."

Dracula hesitated. "I don't know anything about Cowen, and I doubt my roommates do, either. The most I know about him is what's in the box he left behind."

Every word sounded genuine, but I wasn't ready to accept we'd hit a dead end. If only he'd given me a reason to beat the answer out of him…

I think I enjoyed confronting vampires a little too much. If I treated humans half as bad as I treated vamps, I'd already have my ticket to Hell in hand. I was about to give up and let the vamp go, ready to call this mission officially a bust, when Venn quickly stepped in.

"Do you still have the box?" he asked in a rush.

Dracula's jaw tensed. He was totally over this interrogation. "I might know where it is."

"We'll buy it from you," Venn offered.

The vamp's eyes lit up in intrigue.

"How much do you want for it?" Venn asked.

"I don't want money," Dracula declined, his silver eyes staring greedily at me.

Seriously? Another lonely bastard looking for a good time? He'd be sorely disappointed.

"What *do* you want?" Venn asked.

Either he was dumb or blind. It was obvious by the way the guy eyed me like a piece of meat. *I* was his price.

Screw him. Wait, no. Not what I meant.

"I just want a taste," Dracula said, like it wasn't a big deal.

He can shove his offer—wait... a taste? As in, my blood? Okay, not as bad as I thought, but still...

"No," I answered automatically, my voice filled with disgust.

"Then I think we're done here." Dracula reached for his door handle.

"Wait!" Venn insisted, catching the door again before he could close it.

Dracula looked up with a sardonic smile. "You seem to really want that box."

Venn hesitated.

What was Venn hiding? He *did* really want that box, but I wasn't sure why. He didn't think the thing Cowen stole from him was in there, did he? I mean, this vamp said Cowen had left here years ago. Unless he thought there might be something in there that could help us track Cowen down.

Tracking...

Of course! A tracking spell required an object belonging to the person you were trying to locate. We could use anything in the box to track Cowen, as long as no one else had claimed ownership of the objects inside since he'd abandoned them.

"I lied," I said quickly. "I'll do it."

The vamp smirked the same time Venn spoke.

"No, Rae," he objected. "You don't have to."

"I do," I countered. "We need that box."

Venn whirled toward Dracula. "Feed on me instead."

The vamp stood in the grass beside the curb and shut his car door behind him. He shook his head. "No. I named my price, and I asked for the girl."

His nostrils flared, inhaling my scent—not that he could

smell me well considering I was a shifter. He must've *really* had a thing for female shifter blood. That wasn't surprising, though, since shifter blood tasted best, or so I'd been told. Vampires could feed on animals, but I'd heard it compared to the taste of dirt and the energy boost of an ice cube when you're craving a double bacon cheeseburger. Human blood did the job, but it was like eating salad when shifter blood was a triple-layer chocolate cake with ice cream on top. Vampires didn't get many chances to drink shifter blood since most of us weren't up for donating it. Not to mention that shifter blood slaves were rare. Vamps only took the ones who couldn't fight them off.

I took a step back to distance myself from him. Dracula looked two seconds away from pouncing on me and sucking me dry. He almost had me second-guessing the deal, but then I reminded myself what would happen if I refused. We really would hit our dead end, and I'd be no closer to finding Jenna than I was the night the Soulless took her.

"I'll do it," I said, "but you only get five seconds—"

"A minute," the vamp countered.

"You'd have me drained dry! Five seconds," I replied firmly.

"That's barely a sip!" he complained, like I was being totally unfair.

Frankly, I thought I was being awfully generous for a box of junk that didn't even belong to him.

"Thirty seconds," the vamp negotiated.

I crossed my arms. "Ten, and that's my final offer."

His eyes locked on my jugular as if he could hear my blood pulsing through my veins. I knew he couldn't, not like he could with humans.

Finally, he scoffed. "Forget it. I can buy blood for less than that box of crap is worth."

"You and I both know that my blood fresh from the source is a heck of a lot more valuable than what it sells for at a blood bank," I countered.

Blood from the blood banks was like eating that chocolate cake after it'd sat on the counter for three days—dry and stale. He knew my offer was well worth it.

"Rae," Venn said sternly, trying to talk some sense into me, but I'd already made up my mind. We needed something of Cowen's to track him down.

Dracula's lips tightened. "Fine," he caved. "Ten seconds." He stepped forward and reached out for me.

I quickly dodged out of the way. "Whoa. We get the box first."

Dracula glanced to Venn, as if to ask, *Is this girl for real?*

"And if you try anything," I warned, "you're dead. If you release venom, take longer than your ten seconds, *anything…* my friend here will make sure it's the last drink you ever take."

Dracula gritted his teeth. "Yeah, I get it. No tricks."

"Rae, come on," Venn protested, his voice growing harsher with each passing second. "We'll find another way."

I ignored him. We might find Cowen eventually through other means, but this was our quickest option. "Let's do this," I said to Dracula, sealing our deal.

"No," Venn demanded like I didn't have a choice. He grabbed me by the arm and pulled me away from Dracula.

On instinct, I ripped my arm out of his grasp and swung my fist at his nose. He stumbled backward from the impact, his hands immediately covering his face.

"Damn, Rae," he said with a mixture of anger and amusement in his tone. "You have one helluva swing."

Dracula laughed, but I ignored him. I wasn't amused in the slightest.

"Let's make something explicitly clear," I said, my eyes trained on Venn's. "Just because I asked for your help does *not* mean you own me. I'm doing this on my own, so you can either stay and help or leave without answers."

Silence settled over the lawn.

A muscle fluttered in Venn's jaw as he considered my words. Finally, his shoulders relaxed. "I'll stay."

Dracula smiled triumphantly. "The box is in the garage."

He gestured for us to follow him, but my feet remained firmly planted in the grass. Venn didn't move, either. Dracula glanced back and frowned, like he didn't have all night.

"I said no tricks," I told him.

"This isn't a trick." The vamp sounded annoyed. "I'm upholding my end of our deal."

Maybe he was telling the truth, but how could I trust that there wouldn't be twenty vampires hanging out in the garage waiting for us?

"Bring the box out here to us," I demanded.

Dracula shook his head, like I was being completely ridiculous.

"Do you want my blood or not?" I asked. The truth was I'd follow him into that garage if I had to, but I hoped it didn't come to that.

"Fine," the vamp sighed. "Wait here."

He hurried off toward the side of the garage, leaving Venn and me alone on the dark sidewalk.

I turned to Venn, who stared after Dracula with a hard expression. "He's not coming back, is he?"

"That, or he's bringing a bunch of vamps back with him,"

Venn said. "We should leave before he comes back. This is a bad deal."

"No," I insisted. "We need that box to track Cowen. Don't you want to save Sondra?"

Venn hesitated. Before he had a chance to answer, Dracula had already emerged from the garage. He carried a white cardboard box not much bigger than a paper grocery bag.

Maybe there are vampires out there worth their word.

Dracula dropped the box beside Venn's feet. It landed with a *smack* on the sidewalk.

That was… too easy. We could've just walked in there ourselves and taken it. A minor breaking and entering charge was nothing, and I wouldn't have to give up my blood for it.

I stared into the silver eyes of this Dracula-Cowen look-alike, praying to God—or Synchrony or whatever—that he'd keel over and die right there so I wouldn't have to go through with this. But I knew praying wouldn't do me any good.

"I'll take my payment now," Dracula said, licking his lips.

My skin crawled, and every fiber of my being told me to take the box and run, but I found myself stepping toward him anyway. I wasn't the type of person to go back on my word. I know… shocker. Rachel Collins actually had morals.

But when Dracula took my wrist in his cold hand, I wasn't sure I could go through with it. Suddenly, I wanted to hurl.

I hope my blood tastes like horse shit.

"Wait!" Venn couldn't take it. He threw himself between us, forcing Dracula's hand off mine. "Don't, Rae. You don't want to become a blood slave, believe me."

"Hey!" Dracula rose his voice and shoved Venn aside with his elbow. "No one said anything about blood slaves. We had a deal. You're not trying to double-cross me, are you?"

Venn held Dracula's gaze, his lips tight and nostrils flaring, but he couldn't come up with a rebuttal.

"Are we going to do this or not?" Dracula's teeth gritted. He looked at me in a way that told me that one way or another, he *would* receive his payment.

"Venn, I told you this was my deal," I said.

"Watch out," Dracula warned. "You don't want to get punched by a girl again, do you?"

I almost struck Dracula for the insult. I wasn't just some tiny, weak-ass girl, though he had to know that by now.

I placed a gentle hand on Venn's arm. "Ten seconds. That's it. Ten seconds, and it will all be over."

I stepped toward Dracula before Venn could respond. My hands shook. I knew it wouldn't be anything compared to the pain I felt when Cowen stabbed me with vampire venom, but I still wasn't looking forward to vampire fangs sinking into my neck.

Ten seconds. Then we're out of here.

I ignored Venn and nodded toward Dracula.

"Rae—" Venn started, but I didn't hear the rest of what he said.

Dracula wrapped his arms around me possessively, and a sharp pain shot across my neck. My breath hitched, and my entire body tensed.

Ten... nine...

I started counting down in my head, but two seconds in, I'd already lost track of the numbers. It only took a moment for the initial shock to fade and the pain to go away. Instead, a light tingly feeling danced across my skin, melting away all the tension in my muscles. I forgot about Venn's protests, about the fangs in my neck, about the box near my feet that could hold the key to finding Cowen… all that mattered was the feeling of euphoria filling my body.

Had I really only offered this guy ten seconds? If this was what being fed on felt like, he could take me for ten goddamn years. The pleasure only built within my body each passing second. I yearned for more, but I never got a chance to learn what that might feel like.

My mind was instantly pulled back to the present, to the reality that a *vampire was sucking my blood*, when the deafening roar of a massive beast cut through the night.

8

A moment of disorientation overcame me as the fangs in my neck drew away.

"Step away from the girl," a threatening female voice met my ears.

The pressure around my middle disappeared. I hadn't even realized there'd *been* pressure on my body until it was gone. My legs felt like noodles. Without the strength to hold me up, they crumbled beneath me. A pair of strong hands caught me before I slammed to the ground. It took only a split second for my head to clear, as if I'd just broken the surface of a very deep lake and taken my first life-saving breath.

The first thing I noticed was that Dracula had dropped me. He stared with wide eyes at something beyond me and backed away slowly. The faint scent of cinnamon filled my nose, and I realized it was Venn who had caught me.

A second chilling roar filled the air just feet away from me. I steadied my feet and turned to see Ryland in bear form, glaring at Dracula and poised for attack. Fiona had shifted into a fox, and Teagan was ready with her knives out.

This was *bad*. Ryland had to know this wasn't at all what it looked like.

"Wait!" I cried.

I rushed out of Venn's arms and threw myself between Ryland and Dracula. But Ryland was quicker than me. He'd already leapt into the air, his sharp teeth bared toward Dracula's throat. Ryland's massive paws slammed into my chest. I fell to the ground, feeling as if I'd just been hit by a truck. Ryland quickly righted himself and shot me a glare as if to ask if I was insane.

Possibly.

I sucked in a heavy breath and tried to force out an explanation, but the words didn't come before Dracula had already ducked into his car. Ryland rushed forward, and his heavy shoulder connected with the driver's side door. It crumpled like a soda can. Dracula quickly shifted into drive, flipped us the finger, and sped off down the road.

"Ryland, stop!" Venn yelled to get his attention.

Ryland was already racing after the car, but he didn't get far before realizing he'd never be able to keep up with Dracula's increasing speed.

Teagan rushed over to me to help me to my feet. My chest heaved as I struggled to inhale steady breaths, and my head swam in a lightheaded daze. A warm sensation rushed across the skin on my throat. My hand slapped to my neck and came away sticky with blood.

Great.

I pressed hard over the vampire bite to stop the bleeding. My eyes remained fixed on Ryland as he abandoned the car chase and raced back to the lawn. Even in his bear form, he looked *pissed*.

"Ryland," Venn and I said in unison, in a matching tone that said we had a lot to explain.

But we never got a chance. Fiona's scream of terror ripped across the lawn, startling all of us. Venn, Teagan, and I whirled around, only to be met by half a dozen pairs of silver eyes. Six vampires flooded out of the house. The first vamp already had Fiona by her hair. He was tall, with skin as dark as Venn's and arms as big as Ryland's.

Ryland showed no signs of slowing down.

"Ryland, stop!" I shouted.

He was already flying through the air.

I was so over this *act first, ask questions later* thing.

Alpha Vamp dropped Fiona and ducked out of the way before Ryland's claws could catch him. Ryland's massive bear form flew over the top of him and slammed into the petite female vamp behind him.

"Stop!" I screamed again, but no one listened.

The female vamp was already back on her feet. She drew her arm back and smashed it into Ryland's nose. Ryland swiped his paw out at her, but she ducked. Her clothes fell to the ground as her body shrank to the size of a medium dog. There was a distinct pattern to her brown fur. *A wolverine.*

Whoa. I was totally not expecting that. Vampire-shifter hybrids were rare, especially since shifters weren't common in the general population to begin with. Unlike witch magic, vampires kept their shifter magic when they changed.

Venn shifted and sprang forward to defend Ryland. Teagan grabbed a fistful of Ryland's fur and hoisted herself onto his back. In the blink of an eye, one of her knives flew from her hand and landed square in the center of the female shifter-vamp's chest.

Terror entered the woman's eyes, but it was gone a

moment later as the magic keeping her alive left her body and reduced it to a pile of ash.

Me? I was still holding on to my neck, trying not to bleed out the open wounds Dracula had left. I needed to perform a healing spell—and fast.

What's the incantation? Come on, Rachel, you can do this.

I racked my brain, thinking back to the words I'd uttered only earlier today.

The incantation is only four lines. It shouldn't be this hard to remember. Just start somewhere.

I began muttering the first words I could remember. No, that wasn't right. That was the second half of the spell. How did the beginning go?

Three of the remaining vampires had Ryland and Teagan surrounded. Another had chased Fiona up onto the porch, and though the vamp was fast, Fiona was agile enough to avoid getting caught. The vamp was probably a total newbie still getting used to his supernatural speed. Nearby, Venn's wolf claws sank into a vampire's arm. The vampire bared its sharp fangs and hissed.

They need help. I need to get in there.

Suddenly, the incantation clicked. I whispered the four lines from memory under my breath. The moment I finished, Alpha Vamp leapt on top of Ryland and sank his teeth into the back of Teagan's neck. An invisible force slammed into my gut.

"No!" I shrieked.

I didn't have time to check if the spell had taken. I instantly shifted. My clothes dropped away behind me, and I shot into the air, my wings flapping hard. I landed on Alpha Vamp's shoulder and pecked my beak at the first piece of flesh I could find. *His ear.*

Alpha Vamp cried out. His hand shot toward me, but I was already out of reach before his large hands could wrap around my small throat. I flew to the other side of him, and he twisted to follow me. He swatted at me in the air, intent on knocking me out of it. My talons caught him and sliced across the back of his hand. I'd distracted him long enough that when Ryland spun around, Alpha Vamp didn't have time to grab on to any fur. He flew through the air off Ryland's back and landed so hard on the front lawn that his elbow skidded through the grass and left behind a divot.

A quick motion closer to the house caught my eye. I looked just in time to see the vampire chasing Fiona grab ahold of her tail. She shifted back into human form, and her tail disappeared from his grasp. She tried to dodge out of the way, but he was too fast for her. The vampire jumped forward and tackled her to the ground. Her foot flew out and slammed into his nose, but he held her down and climbed on top of her, like he didn't even feel it. The light from the nearby street lamp reflected off his pearly white fangs as they elongated past his upper lip.

Hell no.

I dove toward him, passing through the narrow space between his face and Fiona's neck. He pulled back, startled. I flew in an arc and aimed my body at his face again. He leapt backward, completely disoriented as I flapped my wings in his face over and over again. It was a handy trick. He stumbled back so far that he ran straight into Ryland's backside. Ryland was still trying to fight off two other vampires, and so he didn't even notice when one of his huge back paws stepped on the vamp's foot.

I took the brief opportunity we had to escape. I shifted back into human form and grabbed Fiona's arms to help her to her feet. She followed behind me as I raced across the lawn —in nothing but my enchanted underwear and boots. I scooped up my clothes on the ground and tossed them on top of Cowen's box.

"Come on," I said in a breathless rush as I grabbed the box.

I raced out across the street, and Fiona sprinted behind me. My heart hammered at a million beats per minute once we reached Venn's car. I flung the driver's side door open and tossed the box on the passenger seat. Inside, my hands found the keys Venn had left in the ignition. I twisted, and the car roared to life. I hadn't driven a car in years and didn't have my license, but I remembered enough from my driver's ed class.

I shifted into drive and pressed down on the pedal before Fiona even had the back door shut. Tires squealed when I slammed on the brakes in front of the vampires' house a few doors down from where we'd been parked.

"What—?" Fiona started, but I laid on the horn before she could finish, drowning out her question.

Everyone's heads jerked in our direction.

"Open the door!" I instructed in a rush.

Fiona quickly opened her door and franticly gestured for everyone else to make a run for it. Ryland whirled his head to the side, slamming it against the nearest vampire, who was trying to get on top of him. He broke free of the vamp and barreled his way between two others. Teagan grabbed a handful of fur and leaned over, nearly touching the ground but still holding herself up on his back. While Ryland ran, Teagan scooped her knife up from where it stuck in the ground. Ryland shifted not a moment too soon, and he and Teagan stumbled into the back seat.

"Venn!" Teagan cried in a high-pitched shriek I never would've guessed she was capable of.

Venn raced toward us, but two vampires leapt on top of him at the same time. He clawed at them and managed to slice one of them across the cheek.

I was a split second away from streaking across the lawn in nothing but my undies and kicking some vampire ass when a loud *bang* filled the vehicle. The entire car shook, and my heart jumped into my throat. My head snapped in the direction of movement to find Alpha Vamp perched atop the hood of the car. His silver eyes bore straight through the vehicle to the back seat. He glared at Teagan with a look of vengeance in his eyes.

Not today, buddy.

"GO!" Venn's voice filled my ears from mere feet behind me.

Relief flooded through me when I heard his voice. He was all right—for now, anyway.

Without a second thought, I floored the pedal. Alpha Vamp steadied himself on the hood of the car. In my rearview mirror, I saw four vampires rush out onto the street, following much closer behind us than I would've imagined they could. I swerved to the left, then to the right, almost hitting into a vehicle parked at the curb. I must've missed it by inches.

"The brakes!" Venn shouted.

I immediately applied the brakes, and Alpha Vamp went flying. I was half surprised he didn't splat onto the pavement like a bug against a windshield. A *thud* sounded behind us as the four remaining vamps ran into the back of the vehicle, stunned by the abrupt halt.

"Hang on!" I warned as I wrenched the shifter into reverse.

I whirled around to look out the back window and stomped on the gas. The car jolted as the tires passed over at least two separate bodies. It wouldn't kill the vamps, but it would sure slow them down. Shifting back into drive, I put the pedal to the metal and hightailed it out of there. Alpha Vamp leapt from the middle of the road out of my path. Our speed increased rapidly, and I swerved around a slow-moving vehicle ahead of us on the street.

I didn't pay attention to the vamps behind us. I let Fiona—who was screaming at me to step on it—worry about that. Instead, I focused on not crashing as I turned down another street in an attempt to lose the vamps at our tail. I never even saw the stop sign on the next block, but I sure saw the black sedan I almost t-boned. I pulled the wheel to the left as the driver in the other vehicle slammed on his brakes. I just barely missed him.

On the next block, we broke out from the residential area onto a street with more traffic. I made a sharp right turn, and by some miracle, I managed to slip right into traffic without hitting anyone.

Fiona breathed a sigh of relief. "They're gone."

I slowed to follow traffic, but my heart continued to slam against my rib cage. I glanced back briefly to see that Venn was still trying to get situated, but it was nearly impossible with Ryland taking up half of the back seat. Apparently, Venn decided he had enough of trying to fit four people in the back, because he ducked his head and climbed over the middle console. It took him a good ten seconds of struggling—since there wasn't exactly much room for a guy his size—before he was seated in the passenger seat with Cowen's box on his lap.

"What the hell happened back there?!" Ryland exploded.

I opened my mouth to explain, but before I could, Fiona's small voice cut through the brief silence in the car.

"Um, guys," she said with concern.

"What?" Ryland snapped, like he didn't have time for her.

I glanced to the back seat to see that Teagan's body was slumped against Fiona's, her eyes closed. Fiona slowly drew her hands away from Teagan and stared down at the blood on them in horror.

Fiona shook. "Teagan's not breathing."

9

I was pretty sure *I* stopped breathing when I heard Fiona mutter those words. I wrenched the wheel to the right and slowed to a stop in a gas station parking lot. I kicked my door open and rushed out of the vehicle, still half-naked and everything. I pulled Ryland's door open so fast that I was half surprised it didn't rip off its hinges.

Ryland didn't even notice me there. He leaned over Teagan and shook her, begging her to wake up. Because *that* was totally going to work.

I reached two hands around Ryland's bicep—and they didn't even reach all the way around—and pulled at him. "Move! Let me help her."

It took several tugs before Ryland acknowledged me. Then, as if he suddenly remembered I actually *could* help her, he dropped her shoulders and jumped out of the car.

I climbed into the back seat and knelt over Teagan. The first thing I did was check her chest while Fiona pressed her hands over her wounds. I was relieved to see that it was rising and falling, though slowly.

"She's still breathing. That's a good sign," I said. "Help me, Fiona."

Together, we propped Teagan up in the middle of the back seat.

"What happened to her?" Ryland demanded desperately from outside the car. "Is she going to be okay?"

On the other side of Teagan, Fiona was breathing heavy, shallow breaths, like she was doing everything she could to keep from freaking out.

"How can we help?" Venn asked from the front seat. His head was screwed on straighter than Ryland's, but his tone still sounded rushed and worried—for good reason.

"What's wrong with her?" Ryland's voice rose as he began pacing.

I didn't answer him right away. I reached for Teagan's dark braid and pushed it out of the way. Fiona lifted her hands, exposing the back of Teagan's neck. Two puncture wounds lay side by side on her skin, confirming what I'd seen earlier. My stomach churned at the sight of the raw, swollen skin and the blood soaking into her shirt.

"What?" Venn demanded.

I could hardly get the words out past the lump in my throat, but somehow, I managed. "She's been bit."

Ryland stopped pacing abruptly. "You can help her, can't you?"

I turned to him, hoping the fear I felt for Teagan didn't come across in my expression.

"Can't you?!" Ryland shouted.

I swallowed hard. "I can try."

The truth was, I knew there was nothing I could do. The only spell I had that I thought might help—the one to counteract supernatural injuries—was clearly a dud. But if we didn't do something about that venom, we could be waking up to a vampire in the morning.

"I need that shirt, Venn," I demanded.

Venn tossed me the shirt I'd been wearing earlier.

"How did this happen?" Ryland asked, to no one in particular. "She was with me the entire time."

"That big vampire bit her while she was on your back," I said, wiping the shirt across the blood. "I saw it."

"Is she going to—?" Ryland started, but I cut him off before he could finish.

"No," I told him. "We're going to fix this. But either way, she's going to have a rough night."

"*A rough night?*" Ryland repeated, like he couldn't believe my words. "So you're saying you can't do anything? I thought you could heal!"

"I'm going to do my best!" I shot back at him. "Stand back if you don't want blood all over your shoes."

Ryland's hands shook, like he was trying to physically hold himself back from ripping me out of the car just to hold Teagan in his arms, but he stepped aside anyway.

Peeling the soaked shirt off her back, I took a deep breath to ready myself. The longer I thought it through, the deeper the venom would penetrate into her body. So, ignoring my instinct to brainstorm further solutions, I lowered my lips to her skin and sucked her blood into my mouth.

A fire burned across my lips and raged through my mouth, scorching every millimeter of my body that her tainted blood touched. There was no taste to it; only fire. It was like eating the hottest ghost pepper in the world, if that pepper had been coated in red-hot molten lava.

I longed to cry out, but I resisted the urge. I didn't need everyone worrying about Teagan *and* me. My mouth filled with blood. I turned my head out the open door and spit. Blood sprayed across the pavement. I quickly returned my lips to her wound and repeated the procedure until the pain in my mouth stopped building and became a constant dull, but intense, pain.

"I got most of it," I slurred, my tongue barely able to move in my mouth. "Just need to stop the bleeding."

Before I had a chance, Teagan lifted her head slightly. A small groan escaped her lips.

"Tea?" Fiona asked in a rush.

Teagan only replied by gritting her teeth and letting out another sound of discomfort. I was surprised tears weren't rolling down her cheeks.

"We need to get her home," Venn insisted.

Just as I placed my hand over the bite marks on the back of Teagan's neck, the door beside me slammed closed, making me jump. A second later, Ryland was climbing into the driver's seat. I ignored Ryland's curses and Venn's instructions that he thought were helping. Instead, I focused on channeling my magic into Teagan's skin. On the other side of her, Fiona rubbed her back.

I muttered the incantation two more times just to make sure. Before I could start the incantation a fourth time, Teagan's head snapped upward, and a high-pitched shriek filled the vehicle. I nearly jumped out of my skin. As fast as the screech came, it was gone, and Teagan slumped back against Fiona.

Ryland whirled around in his seat, completely oblivious to the cars in front of him. "What'd you do to her?"

"It's the venom," I bit back. "Eyes on the road!"

Ryland twisted back around just in time to slam on the brakes. He barely missed hitting the car in front of us that had stopped at a red light. Venn braced himself against the dashboard.

"Calm. Down," Venn barked at Ryland. "You're not going to do Teagan any good by getting her killed before we make it home."

The sound of Ryland's heavy breaths filled the car, but he ignored Venn. The light turned green, and the car jerked forward. Ryland weaved between vehicles and sped through a yellow light, then took a sharp left turn.

I wiped the remaining blood away from my mouth and Teagan's back with the t-shirt. I was satisfied to see her swelling had gone down and the bleeding had almost stopped.

Several minutes later, we pulled into the driveway of their home. I jumped out of the car so that Ryland could scoop Teagan into his arms and carry her up to the house. Fiona rushed out of the car behind Ryland.

Finally, I took a moment to breathe. I stared after them. After everything that happened today, I needed a minute to absorb it all.

"Here." Venn's voice cut through the darkness.

I tore my gaze from the house to see him holding my pants and purse in one hand and balancing Cowen's box in the other. He avoided my gaze.

"Thanks," I said shyly as I took the pants from him. I *so* needed to get my own clothes back. Running around half-naked every time I shifted was not high on my bucket list. I held the pants close to my chest, covering up as much exposed skin as I could. I mean, I wasn't exactly showing off more than I ever did at the pool, but still... My off-white underwear didn't exactly scream *sexy*.

I stood there awkwardly, going beet red under Venn's gaze. I wasn't sure if I was supposed to get dressed right here in the middle of their driveway or what. And what was our plan going forward?

"We should get inside," Venn suggested.

The tension in my shoulders eased. At least I had a plan for the next five minutes. After that… I had no idea.

10

I followed Venn into the house. Teagan's cries of pain traveled down the stairs and to the front door.

Venn exchanged a glance with me. "You're sure there's nothing more you can do?"

Fiona's voice came from the top of the stairs before I could answer. "You probably shouldn't even try, unless you want Ryland to bite your head off."

I hated to think that he literally could do just that.

"That bad?" Venn asked.

Fiona descended the stairs and held out a clean shirt to me. "He says Teagan needs space. He's cleaning her up and trying to make her comfortable right now. I think this is harder on him than it is on her."

"She's tough," Venn said.

Fiona stared up at Venn with tears at the corner of her eyes. "She'll be fine, won't she?"

"Yes," I said, hoping to sound reassuring. "I don't know everything about vampire venom, but I know there's not enough in her system to cause long-term damage."

Fiona bit her lip, and her voice cracked. "You're sure?"

"Hey, Fiona," Venn said softly.

He set down the box in his hands and stepped forward to pull Fiona into a hug. She hugged him back, looking comfortable in his arms. It wasn't the type of hug that made me suspect there was something between them. It was more like the type of hug a brother and sister might share.

Still, it didn't feel right to be standing there watching their family moment. I slipped out of the hallway into the dining room, where I finally pulled on the clothes in my hands. Though I wasn't thrilled to still be in Teagan's clothes, I felt a hundred times more comfortable now that everything was covered.

I sensed Venn in the doorway before I saw him. He entered the room looking like he had something he wanted to apologize for. Probably for dragging me into all this, even though I was the one who insisted on coming. He seemed like the kind of guy who would do that.

Fiona followed behind him.

"So..." Venn dragged out the word and glanced down to the box he carried. "Should we check it out?"

I nodded, because my mouth still burned. Apart from the pain, I was running out of strength anyway. How late was it? I was used to staying up late, but tonight, I was completely drained.

Venn sat and set the box in front of him on the table. I sank into the chair beside him. He pulled the top off the box, and together, we leaned forward to peek inside. My stomach fluttered at the close proximity.

I didn't know what I expected to find, but I thought it'd be more... vampire themed, though I had no idea what that would entail. Vials of blood or something? Instead, all we found was a pile of junk: pens, a phone charger, an old watch, a thin roll of duct tape. There was even a pack of mint gum, which seemed weird for a vampire, but I guess when you didn't need to eat regular food anymore, gum was a good way to add flavor to your diet.

I frowned, but inside, I was completely heartbroken. I let a vampire bite me for *this*? This probably wasn't even Cowen's stuff. Dracula could've just grabbed a random box of junk from the garage so that he could get consent for a taste of my blood.

Venn took a deep breath and stood. A curse slipped out under his breath.

"What's wrong?" Fiona asked. She stood behind the chair across from me and looked into the box. "What's with the box anyway?"

Venn raked his fingers through his hair. "It's Cowen's. We were hoping to use it to track him. What you saw... Rae agreed to it as a trade." He shot me a look like he still wasn't pleased about the whole thing.

"You should've called us," she said. "When we went to check out the back, we didn't see anything. Then we heard your voices at the front of the house, and we came to check it out. If we knew what was happening, Ryland never would've—"

"I know," Venn cut her off. "I just saw the vamp, and I didn't think we had time..."

Fiona shook her head like she'd never understand men. She stood on her toes and leaned over the box, shuffling through the random junk. "So, we can use any of this stuff to track Cowen?"

"Probably not," I said. "Tracking spells work best with sentimental objects, but even then they're tricky. We might've had a chance with something else, like a piece of clothing. But this stuff... I don't think it'll work."

"What about the watch?" Fiona asked, holding it up.

I reached for it. "It's worth a shot, but the real challenge is going to be coming up with the money for a tracking spell."

Fiona and Venn both stared at me blankly.

"What?" I asked. "Any witch with a business sense is going to charge us double for asking to track a guy with a watch he abandoned years ago."

"We... um... we don't need to pay a witch, do we?" Fiona asked with hesitation. "I mean, what about you?"

Venn raised his eyebrows, like he agreed Fiona had a point.

"Me?" I asked in disbelief.

"You have a tracking spell, don't you?" Venn pointed out.

"Well, yeah," I said. "I have the spell, but I'm only a low witch."

The corner of Venn's lips turned down. "You know that's not true. No low witch can heal like you do."

"Okay," I agreed, "so I'm on the low end of a mid-witch. I still don't have enough magic to perform this type of spell."

"I don't think you give yourself enough credit," Venn said.

Really? We were back to this again?

"I know what I'm capable of," I snapped. "Witches have *died* trying to access power beyond their capabilities."

"Yes," Venn agreed, "but you can also improve your powers by testing those limits, by practicing magic."

He thought I was being lazy? Like I hadn't *tried* testing my limits before? Because apparently my notebook full of spells wasn't proof that I at least had an *interest* in getting better at magic...

"Do you really think I'd be here right now if I could

perform this kind of spell?" I asked. It wasn't like I hadn't tried. If I could do this, I would've found my sister ages ago.

"You can do it," Venn promised. "You just don't know you can."

"Fine," I said with determination in my voice. "I'll prove it to you what my limits are. Get ready to write a big check, because when you turn to another witch for this, it's not going to be cheap."

"Hold on," Venn protested, but I was already moving Cowen's box off the table.

I pulled my spell book from my bag and flipped open to the tracking spell I'd copied from a book at work.

"You need to—"

"Hey, Fiona," I interrupted without looking at Venn. "Can you get me some salt from the kitchen? Also, I'm going to need a few candles if you have them. Four, at least."

Fiona nodded and hurried into the kitchen.

Venn sighed, like I was being ridiculous. "Rae, this isn't going to work like this."

My eyebrows shot up. "Oh, so you're the spell expert now?"

"No," Venn replied, "but remember what I said about Synchrony? You can't do this just to prove me wrong."

I opened my mouth to counter, but I hesitated. Maybe he was right and I was totally going about this the wrong way. I would've loved to prove him wrong, to show him he had no right to be making assumptions about me, but the truth was that I didn't have time for this. None of us did.

Fiona returned and set a salt shaker in front of me on the table. She found four candles and a lighter in a nearby cabinet and returned to her seat with all of them in hand.

"Okay," I caved. "You seem to know how I *can* do this. What do I have to do to make it work?"

Venn finally relaxed and sank back into his chair. "The first thing is that you have to let go of all that negative energy you're holding."

Yes, because telling me to do that will make it all magically disappear.

"How do you suggest I do that?" I asked.

Venn shrugged.

Great. He doesn't even know.

"How do you normally relax?" he asked.

I kill criminal vampires.

"Ice cream," I said instead, because even though I had no problem killing vampires, I didn't want to come across sounding like an insane serial killer. Ice cream sounded like a safe bet, and I was hungry anyway. Plus, it might help cool the heat on my gums. "Do you have any?"

"I'll get it," Fiona offered.

I returned my attention to Venn. "Once I'm relaxed, then what?"

Venn leaned forward in his chair and laced his fingers together on the tabletop. "We talked about this earlier. You have to perform the spell without doubt. If you're focusing all your attention on how the spell won't work, it will fail every time."

He said it like you could just switch your doubt off at the snap of a finger.

"Okay," I agreed. "I won't doubt myself."

Venn shook his head. "You can't just wish you won't doubt yourself. You have to truly believe it."

I gritted my teeth. He made it sound so easy when it wasn't.

"Clearly, you know I don't think this is going to work," I pointed out. "Why are we even bothering?"

"Because," Venn said, "I still think you can do it. I think, deep down inside, you have the power to become an amazing witch."

The corners of my lips twitched involuntarily. "Keep talking…"

Venn smirked. With enough compliments, I might just believe in what he was trying to tell me.

He leaned even closer until he was just inches away from me. I could smell the scent of cinnamon on his skin and feel the rush of his breath across my arm. My breath hitched, and it took everything I had not to close the distance between us. All I wanted was to touch him.

"I think you've been on your own for too long," he said softly. "And I think that without someone there to believe in you, you forgot how to believe in yourself."

So much for the compliments.

"Wait." Venn grabbed my hand before I could pull away. My skin tingled at the touch, sending warm vibes up and down my arm. "The thing is, it will never matter how much I tell you how beautiful or strong or smart I think you are if you don't feel that way yourself. I can't give you faith. That can only come from inside you. But I will tell you this…" Venn's gaze dropped to my hand as he ran his thumbs over the back of it, sending my heart going haywire and making me forget all about the pain on my lips. "I absolutely believe that you can do this, that one day, you will embrace Synchrony and do amazing things with it."

I scoffed lightly. "You say that like you can predict the future." Which would've been strange, even in our effed-up world.

Venn shook his head. "I don't know the future, but I know you've done amazing things with magic before. Your soul is powerful, Rae, and once you come to realize that, nothing will be able to stop you."

I couldn't help but smile. He was trying a *little* too hard. It was quite amusing.

"What?" Venn asked innocently.

"You think I'm beautiful?" I teased.

Disappointment crossed Venn's face. "*That's* what you got out of that?"

"That, and you can't tell the future."

Venn sighed and dropped my hand. He leaned back in his chair. "All I'm saying is that I believe in you, and *maybe* that's enough magic to make you see it, too."

Oh, wow. He really meant it. He wasn't just telling me what he thought I wanted to hear.

I narrowed my eyes. "I thought you weren't a witch. You don't *have* magic."

He nodded in agreement. "Not like you do."

"Here you go." Fiona set a bowl of vanilla ice cream in front of me, then one in front of Venn.

"Thank you," I said before digging in.

Fiona sat across from me and dipped her spoon into her ice cream. "Is there anything else you need? I mean, for the spell?"

I glanced at the notebook beside me. "Nope, that's it. But according to Venn—" I shot him a glance "—I need to find a little confidence."

"What?" he asked with a mouthful. "It's true."

I rolled my eyes. *Okay, maybe he has a point. It's not like it'll hurt to be open-minded, about Synchrony, about everything. Just try it.*

I sat quietly, letting the ice cream melt in my mouth and focusing on the cooling sensation and sweet flavor. I forced my shoulders to relax and pictured the negative energy in my body melting away with the ice cream. Fiona exchanged a skeptical glance with Venn, but neither of them said anything. I finished my ice cream far too soon, but I thought it would be rude to ask for another serving.

"So, here's how the spell works." I pushed my bowl aside and stood. I placed Cowen's watch at the center of the table, then situated the four candles in a square around it. I popped the top off the salt shaker and emptied the entire contents in a thick circle around the candles. I took the lighter and lit each of the candles.

"Should I get the lights?" Fiona asked.

I shrugged. "It doesn't say anything about lighting, but if you want to, go ahead."

"Will it help you concentrate?" she asked.

I thought about it for a moment, then nodded.

Fiona rose from her chair and flipped off the light switch. In the darkness, it felt eerie to be sitting in a stranger's home performing a spell.

"Now what?" Fiona asked curiously.

I didn't have much to go off of, only my notes on the ingredients needed and the incantation I was supposed to mutter. Beyond that, I wasn't sure how the spell actually worked to track someone down. I just hoped this wasn't another one of Mrs. Carlyle's shoddy spells.

Venn set his bowl aside. "Remember, Rae, you can do this."

I nodded. I just needed to believe in myself, or so Venn said.

I shut my eyes and took a deep breath, letting out the remaining tension in my body on the exhale. *This is going to work*, I told myself. I did my best to shut out the second voice in my head telling me I was wrong. *Just believe. It can't be that easy, can it?*

Finally, I opened my eyes. I spoke the incantation in my notebook, but the words hardly sounded like my own. They sounded strong and confident, and I had no idea if I was doing this just for show or if I truly felt it in my heart.

By the time I reached the end of the short incantation, nothing had happened. Further down the page, my notes read that the incantation needed to be repeated several times.

No giving up, Rachel. You've got this.

A light breeze passed through the room, rolling from the kitchen to the dining room windows and rustling their curtains.

Maybe I'm actually doing something, I thought.

The breeze grew stronger the longer I repeated the words in my spell book. A prideful smile swept across Venn's face, and Fiona shifted in her chair in excitement.

Right in front of my eyes, granules of salt began to swirl together, rising up from the tabletop in a smooth, controlled manner, as if somehow my magic had created a tiny invisible twister on the table.

I held in my urge to cry out and rejoice, to gloat to Venn that I was actually doing it, but I couldn't stop the incantation now. I continued, and my chest filled with a sense of victory. We were going to find Cowen. The thieving bastard was going to get what was coming to him, and I was going to finally get the answer to the question that had been burning inside of me for years.

The remaining granules of salt rose from the table until they all come together to form an orb in the middle of the candle square about a foot above Cowen's watch.

Fiona leaned over to Venn and whispered, "Is that supposed to happen?"

Venn simply held and index finger to his lips, instructing her to stay quiet.

Then, in the blink of an eye, the salt orb exploded, blasting back into my eyes. I instinctively flinched and fell back into my chair, my heart racing.

It didn't work. I failed.

I forced my breathing to slow and the heat to leave my eyes before I opened them. A knot twisted in my chest, but I did my best to hide it.

"Was that it?" Fiona asked, rubbing her eye. "Do you know where Cowen is?"

I gritted my teeth. "Did it look like it worked?"

"I—I," Fiona stammered. "I've never seen this spell done before. I'm sorry."

"Don't be." Regret filled my voice. "It's not your fault. It's mine."

I couldn't keep my anger in any longer. I shot to my feet and raced out of the room.

11

The front door slammed behind me. By the time I was outside, I realized I *really* didn't know what I was doing because I'd left my spell book, my purse, and my good pants behind. I couldn't just leave right now. Well, I could, but then I'd have to come back to retrieve my things later.

Instead, I sank down onto the steps and covered my face with my hands. *Where did I go wrong? I believed in myself like Venn said I should. Maybe he was wrong. Maybe I don't have enough power for this. I'm only a low witch. I'm never going to find Jenna.*

The door creaked open behind me. I *really* didn't want company right now. But apparently whoever had followed me outside couldn't read minds, because they sat on the step beside me. I thought it was Venn and was about to tell him to leave me alone, that I'd be back inside when I was ready, but then Fiona's voice reached my ears.

"Hey, Rae," she said softly. "It's okay. It really is."

I dropped my hands from my face and lifted my gaze to

hers. It was dark out, but it was easy to make out her soft features with the light from a nearby street lamp.

"No," I stated flatly. "It's not okay. We need this to work. If I was a better witch, you'd be closer to rescuing Sondra, and I wouldn't still be wondering if my sister is dead or alive."

Fiona cocked her head. "Your sister? That's what you're doing this for?"

I nodded. I wasn't sure why I opened up to Fiona. Maybe it was my emotions running high and the inherent *need* to talk to someone, or maybe it was because I thought she and her family could help me. Whatever the reason, I found myself telling her things I'd never talked to anyone about before.

"Two years ago, vampires raided our house," I said. "They killed my parents and kidnapped my sister as a blood slave. I tried tracking spells on my own, but they never worked. I turned to a witch the first chance I got, after I saved up enough money, but she couldn't do the spell. She said I'd already claimed ownership of everything I had left of my sister's, so she couldn't use any of that to track her."

The sorrow on Fiona's face deepened the longer I talked.

I dropped my gaze to my hands. "I'd pretty much given up hope trying to find her until… until I met Cowen."

"You think he knows something about your sister?" Fiona asked.

I nodded, and a silent beat passed between us.

"The Soulless took her, didn't they?" Her voice was so soft, so full of sorrow. "That's why you need him?"

I closed my eyes and took a deep breath. "Yeah. I just wish I could do it on my own."

"You're the *Ravenite*," Fiona said in admiration. "You can do practically anything."

I rolled my eyes. "Don't fool yourself. I'm not what they

make me out to be. I've never been good at magic. I work at this magic shop downtown because I thought it would help me get better at magic, but the whole thing is a joke."

Fiona scoffed. "Most of them are."

"My boss is an idiot," I complained. "For one, the shopfront is a bakery, but he'll just leave charms and shit lying around by the donuts. And he basically has no protocols for when people come in the back where I work. He's barely a low witch but sells charms he claims are enchanted with protection spells. He resells spells that barely work, at best. He's a total con artist. I only stayed because I need the money."

Fiona nodded like she understood. God, it felt good to finally talk to someone. And Fiona just sat there listening without judgement. For the first time in years, it felt like I could actually make a real friend. But I didn't let myself entertain the idea. Now was not the time to get distracted.

"Anyway," I said, changing the subject. "I'm really sorry that I can't help you."

"It's not your fault," Fiona replied. "Venn's being too hard on you."

"Thank you!"

Fiona giggled but quickly composed herself. "He can't just expect you to jump into a complicated spell like that. He needs to realize that it takes small steps and a lot of practice."

I frowned. "I have been practicing."

"Right," she said. "That's why you can heal, because you've already done the spell before and know you can. Next, you need to try something just a little bigger, until you know you can do it, rather than jumping straight into something so different."

Fiona made a lot more sense to me than Venn did. You don't just become powerful by *believing* in it. It took practice.

A slight smile spread across my lips. This sounded like the kind of pep talk Jenna would give me.

"So, you're not mad at me?" I asked. "For not being able to perform the spell, I mean?"

"Of course not!" Fiona said. "None of this is your fault."

"But Sondra's still missing," I pointed out.

"Again, not your fault," she said. "I'd blame a hundred different people before I'd blame you."

An uncomfortable silence hung in the air. I dared to break it.

"Whose fault is it?" I wanted to take back the question as soon as I asked it. It wasn't fair of me to ask something like that when I didn't even know Fiona.

She didn't even hesitate to answer. "Matias," she snarled in disgust.

Okay, now I *had* to know.

"Who's Matias?" I asked. "Wait. *Matias Vayne?* The richest vampire in the state? The one who owns like fifteen skyscrapers in Chicago?"

"The one and only," Fiona confirmed. "But you forgot *manipulative and controlling jackass.*"

I chuckled. "Doesn't that apply to all vampires?"

Fiona smirked. "It certainly does. But Matias is worse than most. He has hundreds of supernaturals working for him who basically bow down to him. He'll do anything to maintain his power."

Power was always a dangerous motivator.

After a beat, I spoke again. "So, what happened?"

Fiona turned to stare me straight in the eyes. "First, a little backstory. Sondra's a high witch—the low end of a high witch, but still a high witch. She runs a business collecting and selling magical artifacts—totally underground like your boss does. She does other things, too, like sells protection charms, performs spells, stuff like that…"

"Why haven't I ever heard of her?" I asked. I liked to know what was going on in the magical community. It was one of the other reasons I stayed at my job. There was always gossip running through that place.

"She likes to keep a low profile," Fiona answered. "She's pretty selective about her clientele. A few years back, she was involved with some bad business deals. She ran into a lot of debt with some other witches while she was trying to get her business off the ground, but the interest was so high that we've just been falling further and further behind." Fiona dropped her gaze and pursed her lips. "At this rate, we'll never be able to pay off the debt, even if we sold the house."

My heart broke for her family. It didn't sound like Sondra deserved that.

"Anyway, Matias offered us a job." Fiona spoke slowly, like the story was about to get really bad. I held my breath, bracing for it. "The money he offered us would've been enough to pay off the debt. We could've even moved out of the city. All any of us really want is to lead a quiet life, maybe use our magic to do some good in the world."

Fiona sighed. "We spent months looking for this artifact he wanted to pay us for. We even had to ask for more time, and Matias let us have it. But… then Cowen came along."

"Venn told me he stole something from you," I said solemnly.

Fiona nodded. "It was the Leora Locket. It's a magical artifact named for the witch who created it. As the story goes, the owner of the locket can use it to predict the future."

I narrowed my eyes. "Why are you telling me this? I mean, if I find Cowen, I could just take it and run."

"For one, I don't think you're like that," Fiona answered.

"You don't even know me," I pointed out.

"I know," she said, "but I just feel like I can trust you. Besides, the locket isn't as great as it sounds."

I cocked my head. "How so?"

"It can only *predict* the future, but the future can still be changed," Fiona explained. "The locket was created using a spell designed to connect the wearer with the spirit realm so they could communicate with loved ones—"

"Wait," I stopped her. "The spirit realm? We're talking about *ghosts* now?"

Though I was shocked by Fiona's mention of ghosts, it shouldn't be so hard to believe after everything else I'd seen in the last eight years.

"Not *ghosts*, exactly," Fiona said, "but yeah. Anyway, the locket became connected with Synchrony—you know what that is, right?"

I nodded. "Venn explained it."

"Right. So, Synchrony is connected to everyone, and so it can see other people's intentions. The locket detects that and shows you how the events would play out."

"That still sounds useful," I said.

"Oh, sure," Fiona agreed, "but intentions can change, and you have to know whose future you're looking into for the locket to work. But someone else's intentions might get in the way of that future. Matias wants power, and he thinks the Leora Locket will give him that, but it really can't. There are too many factors at play."

"So, you're conning him?" I asked, slightly amused.

"No," Fiona stated flatly. "We're doing the job he asked us to do."

"But you didn't tell him about the locket's limitations," I pointed out. "Why tell me?"

Fiona paused. "I don't know. There's just... something about you."

The way she looked at me, it was like I was supposed to know what she meant, but I was only confused.

"Anyway," Fiona continued. "Cowen knew some stuff about the locket, and we ended up turning to him for answers. Once he knew what we were after, he waited until we got our hands on it, and then he stole it. Needless to say, Matias was *not* happy. After already granting us more time, he wasn't exactly inclined to wait any longer."

"So he kidnapped Sondra," I guessed.

Fiona pursed her lips and nodded. "She went to have a meeting with him, and he wouldn't let her leave. He's using her as collateral to motivate the rest of us to deliver the locket."

My chest felt empty. I hadn't even met Sondra, and here I was feeling like I'd lost her, too.

"Do you think she's okay?" I asked in a whisper.

Fiona didn't answer right away, as if she wasn't quite sure what she thought. "She better be. Otherwise, Matias isn't getting anywhere near that locket."

I chewed the inside of my lip, hoping I'd find the right words for her, but nothing I thought of sounded right in the moment. Still, I found the words coming out of my mouth anyway. "We'll get that locket, Fiona. I don't care if we have to sell our kidneys and pay a high witch to track Cowen down." *Not sure why I haven't thought of that before...* "One way or another, we'll find him, and we'll both get back the people we lost."

The door creaked open behind us, and Fiona and I both turned to look. Venn had a frown fixed to his face.

"What is it?" Fiona asked.

Venn sighed, stalling his answer. "I talked to Ryland. We agreed it's time to call Genevieve."

I glanced between the two of them, hoping someone would explain who Genevieve was, but neither of them did.

Fiona stood and pursed her lips. "I was really hoping it wouldn't come to this. We don't have any other options?"

Venn shook his head. "It's too late. I've already called her."

Fiona stared at him in total disbelief, her mouth agape. "Uh… okay. When are we meeting her?"

"In the morning," Venn answered. "We all need to rest. If you want to stay, Rae, we can make up Sondra's bedroom for you."

My heart lifted in my chest, feeling a hundred pounds lighter for a second. "Are you sure?" I asked uncertainly, not wanting to intrude.

"It's totally fine," Fiona assured me. An inviting smile spread across her face.

"Thank you," I accepted, making sure they heard the gratitude in my tone. I didn't feel like going back home to my lonely apartment tonight. "I'm exhausted."

"It's the spell," Fiona said. When I shot her a questioning look, she explained. "Most of the spells you've cast probably haven't drained you because they were well within your abilities. But when you try to cast a spell beyond your abilities, the energy starts to draw from your body instead of Synchrony. Don't worry about it. The more you practice, the more you'll expand your abilities. You'll be able to draw from Synchrony more and more without feeling the drain on your body."

My jaw went slack. "You say that like it's not a big deal. Something like this could kill me!"

"Believe me," Venn said, "you're far from conducting spells that could kill you."

At least that was comforting, but he could've mentioned the whole energy-draining thing before I tried the spell.

"Come on." Fiona gestured for me to follow her. "I'll show you to your room."

12

"You can stay in here," Fiona said, opening the door to the room farthest from the top of the stairs.

She flipped a switch on the wall, and two lamps on either side of the queen bed lit up, bathing the room in a soft glow. The comforter was a dark purple to match the walls, like the color of royalty. Matching curtains with intricate gold patterns stitched into the fabric covered a pair of wide windows that looked out over the front lawn. In the corner sat a table with three plants and four unlit candles. A yoga mat was rolled up beneath it.

"Thank you," I said, inching my way into the room.

Fiona crossed the room to the closet. "I think Sondra might have something you can wear to bed. If you need a shower, there are clean towels in the cupboard in the bathroom."

I figured I'd have to take her up on that offer. I set my purse on the bed and ran my hand across the soft blanket. Part of me felt weird being in someone else's room without them knowing, but another part of me just wanted to crawl under the covers and sleep in a decent bed for once.

"Here you go," Fiona said, handing me a silky black robe. "Let me know if you need anything else."

"I will," I said with a smile.

Fiona left the room, and I heard her footsteps pad down the hall. The house was quiet, and I assumed Teagan had fallen asleep. Normally, the quiet made me uneasy, but in this house, it felt comfortable, peaceful even.

With the silky robe in my hands, I headed to the bathroom. The shower looked inviting. The water was actually warm, and the pipes didn't squeak when you twisted the faucet. The water hit my skin like a soft caress, washing away most of the tension in my shoulders. I stayed under the cascade of water far longer than I needed to.

By the time I stepped out of the shower, the mirror above the sink was completely fogged up. The soft towel I found in the cupboard felt good against my clean skin, but the silk robe felt even better. After drying my hair out, I ran a brush I found on the counter through it, then gathered my dirty clothes.

As I exited the bathroom in a cloud of steam, I caught Venn's eye just as he reached the top of the stairs. He looked surprised to see me, but the corners of his lips lifted into a slight smile. Butterflies danced in my stomach at the sight of him.

"Hey, Rae," he said softly, gazing at me from under dark lashes. "I'm sorry about earlier. Are you okay?"

I nodded. Even though I still felt bad about the unsuccessful spell, the shower had helped calm me down. I felt like I should say something to him but didn't know what.

"Can we do another load of laundry tonight?" I heard

myself say. Apparently, that was the best I could come up with. "The other half of my wardrobe could really use cleaning."

"Yeah, no problem." He gestured for me to follow him.

I softly descended the steps behind him in silence. I tossed my clothes and a bit of laundry soap in the washer, and Venn started the machine.

"Is there anything else you need?" he asked kindly.

Several answers rushed through my mind, but nothing I dared to say aloud to him.

"No, thanks," I replied as we headed back down the hall. "It's so nice of you to let me stay here."

Venn shrugged like it was no big deal. "Don't worry about it. We had the extra bed tonight anyway."

My stomach dropped as I thought of Sondra. It didn't seem fair that I was showering in her house and sleeping in her bed while she was being held captive. But there wasn't exactly any more I could do to help tonight.

My gaze drifted to the drawings on the walls as I climbed the stairs. Each was a portrait of a different person. They looked incredibly realistic, down to their stray hairs. It almost looked as if they'd been photographed in black and white. Some portraits looked more modern, but others wore their hair and clothing as if they'd lived centuries ago.

"Are these Sondra's ancestors?" I asked, mostly because I wasn't ready to say goodnight to Venn.

"No," he said simply. "It's history."

"History?" Okay, now he had me intrigued. "History of what?"

"Of magic," he replied. He reached the top of the steps and turned to me with a smile. "Recent magic, anyway."

"What do you mean?"

Venn smirked. "You up for a history lesson?"

It sounded like a challenge. "I suppose I have time."

Venn's smile widened, and he pointed to the portrait on the end. "Here, we start with Elizabeth Martin. Ever heard of her?"

"I don't think so," I said, shaking my head. The name sounded vaguely familiar, but maybe it was just a common name.

I stepped closer to the portrait for a better look. Like the drawing of Venn at the bottom of the stairs, Elizabeth's eyes looked incredibly real, as if she was staring back at me through the photograph. An eerie shudder traveled down my spine. She wore a long-sleeved dress that covered her collarbone, and her hair was fashioned in an elegant updo.

"She was the witch who created Valkas," Venn said, like he knew it for a fact.

I furrowed my brow. "How do you know? I've heard stories and speculation, but no one can actually know for sure where vampires came from."

"Sondra does," Venn stated. "Valkas was the first vampire."

"I know *that*." But that was all I knew. That was all *anyone* knew.

"Well, Elizabeth was the one who created him," Venn said. "Not on purpose or anything. It was a revival spell gone wrong. Valkas came from a very powerful family. He recruited Elizabeth. She believed she was to perform a healing spell. He was very sick, but instead of allowing the illness to take him, he wanted to die and come back to life to show that he could conquer anything, even death. She refused to perform the spell, but he threatened her with her family's death if she didn't comply."

"So he knew about magic before everyone else did?" I asked.

Venn cocked his head, confused by my question. Suddenly, his face softened in realization. "Oh, you think Valkas was changed eight years ago? No. This was *centuries* ago. Magic has always been around. But the people who knew about it before kept it secret."

"Right," I said, remembering something he'd said earlier. "Persecution and all that."

"Yes," Venn agreed. "Valkas changed that when he returned eight years ago and everyone freaked out."

I pressed my lips together. "What happened after he threatened Elizabeth?"

"He gave his blood for the spell, but it went wrong," Venn explained. "He died, and she brought him back to life, but he wasn't quite human anymore. He was overcome with blood-lust and couldn't control his power. His family was scared of what he'd become, and he was hunted. He lost the power he once had. That's why all these years later he wants that power back."

"No one's heard from him in two years," I pointed out. "No one's heard from the Soulless at all. You think he's still out there?"

Not everyone believed he was still around, but no one was able to confirm his death, either. Somehow, I *knew* they were still out there, and I knew they had Jenna.

"I think it's possible." Venn shrugged, then pointed to the next picture on the wall. "That's him."

I hadn't noticed the drawing before because my attention had been so absorbed by Elizabeth. When I looked at him, my mouth went dry. I'd seen pictures of him on TV and online, but it was nothing compared to this picture. Fangs protruded from his open mouth, and he looked as if he was screaming. I could practically hear the fear-inducing howl through the portrait. His eyebrows twisted into an enraged expression, every muscle in his face tense. There was a hunger and a lust for power in his evil eyes that sent shivers down my spine. Seeing him like this, I could actually believe he was responsible for all of the terrible things he'd been accused of. Like all vampires, he was flawlessly beautiful, but I there was something in the drawing that told me to be very, *very* afraid.

"That's what he would've been like right after the spell changed him, back in seventeenth century Europe," Venn explained. "He started changing other people, and vampires spent the next one-hundred years spreading across Europe, then to the rest of the world."

How could Venn know all this? He told the story like it came straight from a history book. I'd never met someone before who didn't show skepticism in the vampire stories they'd heard. No one, as far as I knew, had the truth.

"For a long time, Valkas saw vampirism as a curse," Venn continued. "He couldn't go out in the sun, and so he couldn't show off his power. Years later, he came to terms with the bad things about vampirism and started focusing on how much power he did have, like extra strength and the ability to kill so easily. That's when he started thinking bigger. He's already conquered death. Time to conquer the whole world."

Venn frowned, like the very thought of Valkas disgusted him. "Anyway, for many years, humans and witches alike hunted vampires and tried to eradicate them before their population became too large. But about a hundred years in, vampires began to spread wider and faster. The witches were having a hard time finding the vampires. In the mid-seventeen-hundreds, a husband and wife team, Abigail and Charles

Williams, set out to protect the world from vampires, who were killing humans and causing mass panic."

Venn gestured to the next set of portraits. A beautiful woman who looked to be in her thirties smiled back at me. Beside her in another frame, an attractive man smirked, like he knew something I didn't. The way Sondra drew his eyes looked strikingly similar to Venn's, though they otherwise looked nothing alike.

"How'd they do it?" I asked, completely engrossed in his version of the story. "Protect people, I mean."

"Abigail was a powerful witch, and Charles was human," Venn explained, like he was excited I took interest. "Using wolf's blood, she performed a spell that bound his and the wolf's bodies together."

"A wolf shifter like you," I said with a smile.

"Yes," Venn agreed with a light laugh. "Exactly like me. Charles became the first shifter, meant to combat the vampires. He was able to sniff out vampire lairs in his wolf form, helping them reduce the population. Better yet, the spell incorporated protective magic. That's why vampires can't smell us or hear our heart beats. With the help of their hunter friends, Abigail created several other shifters, each a different animal species with their different strengths. They reduced the vampire population to almost nothing and thought they'd eradicated them.

"Another hundred years passed of shifters hunting vampires, but they couldn't completely take them out. The shifter boom set the vampires back for a while, but then they stopped running around killing for survival and began taking blood slaves. They became more organized and grouped together, growing their numbers in secret. By then, the vampires were in the US. People started to go missing quietly, but no matter how many vampires they killed, the witches couldn't manage to kill them all. A team of witches came together just before Valkas was going to unleash his army of vampires."

Venn pointed to the next row of drawings. My eyes remained fixed on the portraits as I descended the stairs, inspecting each face.

"These were just some of the witches who came together to stop him." Venn stood on the stair above me to look at the sketches. He was so close that I could feel the heat radiating off his skin. I had the urge to lean into him, but I resisted and focused on the images instead. "With the help of the shifter population, the witches were able to take out most of the vampires. But they couldn't kill Valkas."

"So, he went into hiding?" I guessed.

"No," Venn answered. "In 1847, they locked him away in a supernatural prison. That way, he couldn't create any more vampires, the shifters could kill the rest of them, and the mass killings would stop."

I thought about his story. It made so much more sense than the other theories I'd heard—like how vampires and shifters had been created by mad scientists, which didn't explain our magic. I'd been mostly accepting the theory that magic came from an alternate universe, but trying to follow the parallel universe theory hurt my head. So far, I was really digging Venn's story.

"The thing is, something went wrong with the spell," he continued.

"Something that affected magic?" I asked. It only made sense.

He nodded.

"So, magic got trapped in the supernatural prison with him?" I guessed.

"Not exactly," Venn clarified. "Magic is all around us, all the time. Always has been. Somehow, the spell took away our ability to *access* magic. We're just not entirely sure why."

"Any theories?" I asked, sensing he might have one or two up his sleeve.

Venn shrugged. "The thing about a spell like that was that it required so much magic that the witches had to work together. There's strength in numbers, after all. But the more people you have trying to accomplish one goal, the trickier it is to carry out. My guess is that not everyone was working together as well as everyone hoped. Synchrony didn't know how to respond. But to wipe out access to magic completely... that's huge. It never could've happened without so many witches participating in the spell."

"What happened while he was trapped?" I asked. "Everyone just forgot magic existed?"

"Basically," Venn said. "Many generations passed, and as technology advanced, most people wrote it off as legend, as make-believe. But the stories of magic were still around, just twisted in different ways. I mean, you knew what magic was before you ever saw it, right? And there's always been a small community of people who still believed magic existed. It's just that most people didn't want to listen until they saw it with their own eyes. Even then, people denied it. They still do."

Don't get me started on those whack-jobs.

"So when he escaped, our ability to access magic returned?" I asked. *Obviously.* "Shifters started shifting, witches started... witching."

Venn laughed. "Yeah."

"You seem to know a lot about this," I stated. "Any idea how he actually escaped?"

Venn shook his head regrettably. "No, unfortunately. That one's still a mystery."

A beat passed between us as I considered his words. I was all too familiar with the rest of the story. Once Valkas showed up, mass panic ensued. Not only was Valkas and his army of new vampires slaughtering, changing, and kidnapping thousands of people like they were trying to win a record on terrorism, but now a bunch of people were discovering they had powers. Everyone was afraid. Afraid of the vampires. Afraid of the shifters. Afraid of themselves. I understood the fear—and the equivalent thrill—because I'd lived through it. The civil rights movement, the blood banks, the new laws, and all of that followed shortly afterward until supernaturals were forced to either suppress their nature or unlawfully succumb to it.

"Is there a history book or something that explains all this?" I asked. "How did Sondra get so detailed with these portraits?"

Venn shook his head. "No history books. She remembers."

Hold up. She remembers? How's that possible?

"Anyway," he said with a yawn before I could ask. "It's getting really late, and we should get some sleep before we meet up with Genevieve in the morning."

"Who *is* Genevieve?" I asked. "How can she help us?"

Venn dropped his gaze, like there was something about Genevieve she didn't want to tell me. "She's a witch," he finally said. "But an… unconventional witch."

My jaw practically dropped. Venn didn't have to say anything more. Somehow, I knew by the look in his eyes that we were about to meet up with a witch who practiced dark magic.

13

Genevieve wasn't just into dark magic. She was into dark *everything*.

The next morning, Venn, Fiona, and I walked up the steps to a large house with dark stone and a black roof. Teagan was feeling better but still not back to normal. Ryland had insisted on staying back at the house with her, so it was just the three of us.

A tall, thin woman answered the door. She looked old enough to be my mother, but her skin was smoother than Fiona's. I was willing to bet she had an anti-aging spell up her sleeve. Her hair was jet-black, in stark contrast to her pale skin. It was short and stuck up at every angle, but in a way that looked like it belonged in a fashion magazine. Her brown eyes were outlined in a dark layer of makeup, and her black dress was made almost entirely of lace.

Genevieve, I presume.

"Come in," she offered in a cold tone. She turned on her heel and started down the hall, leaving the door open behind her.

I warily stepped through the door behind Venn. Inside, the lights were dim. The dark gray walls housed black and white images of random landscapes. At the end of the hall sat a Victorian-style chaise covered in black fabric. The only pop of color was a deep red throw pillow on top of it.

Genevieve led us into a room at the end of the hall. The room was dark, like the rest of the house, but was small and cluttered. Black curtains covered the window. They let in only enough light to make out the shadows in the room. A bookcase spanned one wall. Books without names on their spines lined the bottom shelves, looking old and tattered. On the upper shelves were hundreds of jars of all different sizes. Some held various colors of liquid, while others looked to house different types of herbs and spices. Against the other wall, unlit candles lined the top of a long dresser, surrounding an open book that looked centuries old. I figured it was just for show, but it intrigued me nonetheless.

In the center of the room sat a round table with four chairs and a crystal ball in the center. That *had* to be for show, because as far as I knew, crystal balls didn't actually work. All the room needed was a skull and a cauldron for decoration and you'd be ready for Halloween—not that anyone celebrated Halloween anymore. It'd become far too real and horrifying.

Genevieve raised a thin, dark eyebrow at Venn. "I understand that you'd like me to perform a tracking spell."

"Yes," Venn said with a nod.

Genevieve pursed her lips. "You're well aware that I require payment up front."

The way she said that… it was like they had history together, like she'd given him chances before and wasn't about to put up with any more crap. Not that I could picture Venn giving *anyone* crap—unless for a good reason.

"Of course." Venn didn't look Genevieve in the eye. Then again, neither did me nor Fiona. The woman made my skin crawl.

Venn reached into his jacket pocket and placed a pile of cash and a vial of red liquid in front of Genevieve.

Blood. Venn's blood. Shifter blood.

Not only was it illegal to sell blood anywhere but a government-approved blood bank, but it was *definitely* illegal to sell shifter blood. Devin didn't even deal with shifter blood, and he dabbled in some questionable things. There weren't very many spells that used shifter blood for good, none that I knew of, anyway. But that wasn't saying much.

Genevieve swiped her payment from the table and turned to a small hutch behind her, where she slipped the money and blood into the top drawer.

"Please, take a seat," she said without turning to us.

We did as we were told without muttering a single word. I sat across from where Genevieve stood, while Fiona took the chair on my left and Venn sat to my right.

"How's Sondra doing?" Genevieve asked with her back to us as she reached into a cupboard. She didn't sound the least bit interested in Sondra's well-being. It almost sounded like she was mocking Venn and Fiona.

Fiona clenched her fists, like she'd really like to take a swing at Genevieve. On the other side of me, Venn's jaw tensed.

"You know we wouldn't be here alone if she was fine," Venn said with a hint of malice to his voice.

"Of course not." Genevieve turned around, an attempt at a smile fixed to her face. "Shall we get started?"

She snapped her fingers, and the crystal ball on the table rose into the air. It hovered across the room and landed softly on another table. Six candles floated over to take its place on the black tablecloth. They neatly arranged themselves into a circle.

"*Ardeat ignis*," Genevieve muttered. The candles lit on her command, licking tall flames into the air.

My palms grew clammy. Every fiber of my being told me to run, to get as far away from this place as possible, but I remained rooted in my chair. I didn't come here just to leave without answers.

Genevieve took a large glass jar of salt and poured it in a circle around the candles. She set the jar on the hutch and then gracefully slid into the chair across from me.

"You have the watch we discussed on the phone?" she asked Venn, holding out her palm toward him.

Venn quickly dug into his pocket and placed Cowen's watch in her outstretched hand. She dropped the watch into the center of the table, eyeing it like it was infected with germs. Fiona glanced to me as if I should know what was going on, but I had no reassurances to give her.

My mouth went dry. Part of me was excited to see how this spell would actually work, but another part of me feared that it wouldn't.

Genevieve began chanting under her breath. Her words were the same I spoke last night, but they were different, too. She pronounced them with an accent, making the spell sound more mysterious and... authentic.

I tried not to breathe as the salt rose above the table, afraid that just the smallest breeze might throw the granules out of the air. The candle flames licked higher, something that hadn't happened when I'd tried the same spell last night. The salt swirled above us, spinning faster and faster until it all came together to form a tightly compact ball the size of my fist.

And this is the part where it explodes, where we fail.

On cue, the salt ball burst, as if someone had shot a bullet through it. I flinched away, expecting the granules to assault me, but I never felt a thing. Slowly, I peeled my eyes open.

The salt had stopped a mere foot from my face. The granules had expanded outward to create a ball at least three feet in diameter. They moved in unison, twisting around an invisible axis like a globe. Colors flashed inside of the ball. It took me a second to realize the colors made up real images, as if there was a hidden projector somewhere in the room using the spinning salt granules as a screen. The images flickered by so fast that they were almost impossible to make out. I caught a glimpse of Cowen's face and then the bar we'd tracked him down to, Red Whiskey. Several more images passed by quickly, but they were too hard to see, like we were speeding down a road at an insane, inhuman speed.

The images slowed to settle on an old mansion. Perhaps *mansion* wasn't the right word. It was more like a castle. It was beautiful, with a huge fountain on the front lawn and three big towers reaching into the sky. A security wall ran the perimeter of the property. Beyond that lay a lush green forest.

The image disappeared almost as quickly as it came. In the blink of an eye, the salt stopped spinning and dropped out of the air. Salt littered the table, the floor, and my lap. I sat there speechless, unable to believe the level of magic I'd just witnessed.

Fiona had an expression of sheer terror fixed to her face. She stared across the table at Venn, barely even breathing. Venn cursed heavily under his breath, and his nostrils flared. He looked like he was about to go on a rampage. Somehow, he managed to keep his temper under control, but it was clear that something had *seriously* hit his enraged button.

Genevieve laughed lightly, but it sounded less like she was actually amused by something and more like she was taunting us. "I should've known. What kind of trouble have you gotten yourself into this time?"

Venn shot up from his chair and snatched the watch from the center of the table. "That's none of your business."

"I'm only trying to help, darling," Genevieve replied in a smooth voice, but it sounded fake.

"Yes," Venn agreed, "but we've already paid for all the help we can afford."

Genevieve rolled her eyes and sighed. "Fine. If that's all you wanted, you can help yourself out."

I had no clue what was going on here, but when Fiona stood, I followed behind her. Venn waited until we were both out of the room before turning from Genevieve, as if he wanted to make sure we were both okay before leaving. Nobody spoke as we made our way down the long hall. My stomach dropped further and further with each step I took. I *had* to know what those images meant. Something told me they were bad. *Very* bad.

But I didn't speak, not until we escaped Genevieve's house and could no longer hear her laughter echoing down the hall. I managed to keep my mouth shut until I climbed into the passenger seat of Venn's vehicle.

Finally, I burst. "What happened? What did those images mean? You know where to find him, don't you?"

Venn's jaw remained tense. He didn't meet my eyes as he turned the ignition and shifted into drive. "Yeah," he finally said. "We know where to find him."

"Where?" I asked desperately. "What aren't you guys telling me?"

"You didn't recognize the mansion?" Fiona asked in a small voice.

"No," I replied. "Should I?"

Fiona cleared her throat. "Ever heard of Maliya Valerik?"

I drew in a sharp breath. "Please don't tell me that's who I think it is."

I'd heard whispers. Devin had let the name slip once when he was talking with a client. But he never talked about vampire politics with me. He always shrugged me off when I asked him what he knew.

"If you think she's one of the most powerful vampires in all of Nocton, you'd be correct," Venn said, never taking his eyes off the road.

"That last image we saw… that was her mansion," Fiona explained. "Which means that's where we'll find Cowen. And wherever we find Cowen, we find the locket."

Venn growled in frustration, startling me. "I should've known he was one of them."

"One of who?" I demanded, glancing between Fiona and Venn. "Will someone *please* fill me in."

"Maliya runs her own vampire nest," Fiona explained. "She's recruited hundreds of vampires to do her bidding for her, and they're always the worst of the worst."

"What kind of bidding?" I asked, fearing the answer.

Fiona's skin paled. "Maliya's in the blood slave trade."

My heart stopped. Maliya was basically a pimp. A drug dealer and a pimp. She was likely guilty of the most inhumane things possible. Theft. Abduction. Rape. Murder. It made me nauseous just thinking about it. There was a reason I didn't agree that vampires deserved a trial. Vamps like Maliya didn't belong in this world.

"Why hasn't anyone done anything about it?" I demanded.

"Because she's smart." Disgust filled Venn's tone. "No matter how many times they investigate her, they never find enough evidence to try her."

"But there have to be witnesses!" I insisted.

"Of course there are," Venn agreed, his eyebrows tight. "But talking to the police is a death sentence for a blood slave. Do you really think any of them will talk?"

I didn't answer. Venn had a point.

"If Cowen's working for Maliya, do you think he stole the locket for her?" Fiona asked Venn.

Venn's fists tightened around the steering wheel. "He must've. The vamps who work for her worship her." He sounded hopeless.

"We'll get it back," I said in determination. "We'll crash the nest, find Cowen, and get your locket back."

I twisted in my seat to look at Fiona, but she bit her lip in uncertainty. I glanced to Venn, waiting for him to agree with me. He just stared straight ahead at the road, looking furious.

"What?" I demanded. "That's the next logical step, isn't it?"

"No," Venn said in a clipped tone, but he didn't care to elaborate his blatant disregard for the idea.

"If we're going to run straight into a vampire nest, we might as well forget about the locket," Fiona said. "We could just break into Matias's and rescue Sondra instead."

Except you're forgetting one thing...

I hated that that was where my mind went first, that *I* needed to get into Maliya's to face Cowen. Obviously if they had the choice between helping me and rescuing Sondra, I was clearly lower on their priority list. But still... I felt an incredibly selfish need to convince them to reconsider.

Venn and Fiona sounded hopeless, but I was still determined as ever. Come hell or high water, I was tracking down the Soulless. And that started with crashing Maliya's vampire nest.

14

"**I**'m leaving."

The words didn't sound right coming out of my mouth. They *should've* felt perfectly natural. I hardly knew Venn or Fiona, so what was this guilty sensation doing in the pit of my stomach?

"Leaving?" Venn's face paled.

We stood on his porch. Fiona had already gone inside, but I couldn't bring myself to join the family. We couldn't help each other anymore. I'd managed on my own for years, and one way or another, I'd manage this alone as well.

I shrugged. "Yeah, I mean, you have to go rescue Sondra. I have to find Cowen. This weekend has been fun…" *If you can call it that.* "…But I have work tomorrow, and—"

"Rae, we haven't made any decisions yet," Venn said, like I was crazy to consider leaving. "I told you I'd help you."

"I know," I replied, "but you've already helped. I can figure the rest out on my own."

"No," Venn said sternly.

I took a step back and crossed my arms. "You don't think I'm strong enough to handle myself?"

"That's not what I meant," he insisted. "I'm not going to go back on my word. I want to help you."

"I told you I'm not a damsel in distress," I reminded him. "I don't need a knight in shining armor."

Venn laughed so loud that it caught me off guard. "Believe me, I'm no knight."

No, of course he's not.

I didn't *want* to leave. For the first time in years, I'd met people I could actually get along with. But there were more important things in life than friends.

"Come inside," Venn suggested. "We'll get everything figured out."

"No," I protested with a sigh. We no longer shared a common goal. There was no solution. "I'll just slow you down. Besides, I have nothing to offer you. I can't even cast a decent spell, so I'm not sure why you want me around—"

"Is that what you really think of yourself?" Venn asked.

He stepped forward to close the distance between us. He stood only inches from me. My breath suspended in my chest, but my heart *pitter-pattered* against my rib cage. What *was* it with my body lately? It totally betrayed me every time Venn got within inches of me.

"You think we don't want you here?" he asked.

I couldn't look into his eyes—his gorgeous dark brown eyes. "Well, yeah. Why would you? We barely know each other."

Venn reached up to brush the hair out of my eyes. His touch was like a warm summer breeze across my skin. Calming. Inviting. Desirable. Damn it all if I didn't welcome the gesture. I caved and looked up at him. He gazed down at me with a soft expression, like he was looking into the eyes of someone he knew, someone he felt comfortable around.

My mouth grew dry the longer I stared up at him. I didn't know what it was about the way he looked at me, but it made my fingers quiver and my knees grow weak. Something in his eyes tugged at my heartstrings, making me feel at home—like this was where I was meant to be.

Was it Synchrony talking?

Don't be ridiculous, Rachel. It's called lust.

Venn glanced down at my fingers with a look in his eyes that said he wanted to take my hand in his. I suddenly felt myself itching to accept that offer, but he didn't make the move. Maybe he thought it was too soon for that type of physical contact. To be fair, it *was* too soon for… pretty much anything. But I still felt like I should be melting into his arms.

It'd been *way* too long since I had a boyfriend.

"Please don't leave yet," Venn begged. "At least stay for food."

Was this guy a mind reader or something? Because in my book, free food was always a good reason to stick around. Somehow, he knew exactly what to say to make me reconsider. But still, the stubborn part of me refused to accept. If I stayed, I wasn't sure I'd ever leave.

"Teagan's a great cook," Venn pressed. "You won't regret it."

Damn Venn with his temptation of a home-cooked meal. It totally beat another afternoon of peanut butter and jelly sandwiches.

"Okay," I caved. "I'll stay for lunch, but after that, I really do have to go home. I can't stay."

"I know," Venn said, but it didn't sound like he was actually agreeing with me. It was more like he was just telling me what

I wanted to hear. Venn turned and opened the front door. He stepped aside so that I could enter first.

He might not be a knight in shining armor, but he sure is a gentleman.

The sound of voices in the kitchen caught my attention, and Venn gestured toward the back of the house. We crossed through the dining room and stopped in the doorway to the kitchen. The delicious smell of lasagna filled my nose.

"It's true?" Ryland asked Venn. He leaned against the counter with his arms crossed. "Cowen took our locket to Maliya?"

Venn nodded. "That's where Genevieve tracked him down to."

Teagan peeked into the oven door and then slammed it. I was glad to see she was doing better, but she still looked pale.

She pulled off her oven mitts and threw them on the counter. "I can't believe this!"

"I say we're better off launching a rescue mission into Matias's," Fiona said.

Ryland frowned at her. "And if we're caught without the locket, we're all dead."

"We're dead if we try to get the locket from Maliya, too," Fiona countered.

Teagan looked deep in thought. "Not necessarily."

Wait. They were still going after Cowen?

"What do you mean?" Venn asked.

The anger etched on Ryland's face melted away, like he was catching on to what Teagan was saying.

"Wouldn't they see us coming?" I blurted.

Everyone turned to look at me.

"I mean, because they have the locket," I explained. "It can predict the future, can't it?"

Venn shot me a questioning glance, as if to ask how I knew about it at all, but then he looked to Fiona in realization.

"They wouldn't see us coming," Ryland answered. "Not unless they were watching for us."

"Which they could be," Venn pointed out. "They know we want it back."

Fiona threw her hands up in the air and sighed, as if she was *so* done with everyone's crap. "And this is why we don't have a chance."

"Matias's security is twenty times stronger," Ryland said. "From the moment we step into the building, there will be eighty floors between us and Sondra. Not to mention the cameras on all floors, security guards, restricted areas... The list goes on." He turned to Venn. "You've said yourself Maliya's place is in serious need of a security update."

"Yeah," Venn agreed, "but who needs a security upgrade when no one's stupid enough to break in?"

"Not to mention that we already know our way around Maliya's mansion," Ryland continued, like he hadn't heard him.

I stood silently, wanting so badly to agree with Ryland but not sure if I had a place in the conversation. If we didn't make it to Maliya's, I would never get a chance to confront Cowen.

Venn's jaw tightened. "You can't be serious. We're not doing this."

"Oh, really?" Ryland challenged, straightening. "And I suppose you're going to stop us?"

Venn scoffed. "If you want to run straight into an active vampire nest, be my guest. But we both know you need me to navigate the mansion, and I'm not helping."

"Fine," Ryland said with a shrug. "We'll go without you. Of course, that makes our chances of survival very slim, but—"

"Stop it, Ryland," Venn demanded. "I know you're bluffing. I'm not an idiot."

"You're acting like an idiot!" Ryland boomed, making me jump.

"Calm down, love," Teagan said, reaching for him.

Ryland shrugged her off without even looking at her. His eyes were still trained on Venn beside me. "I mean it. What's your plan, Venn? Leave Sondra to rot in Matias's tower? You know he won't let her go without getting what he wants. And if we don't show up with it, he'll force her to work for him or kill her. Or are you planning to barge into one of his highly-secured skyscrapers and bust her out without anyone noticing? We can't handle Matias on our own, but we *can* handle Maliya. Besides, once we hand off the locket to Matias, it's not our problem anymore. Maliya will go after him, and Matias will let Sondra go free."

"You really think that?" Venn asked flatly. "You know Maliya doesn't play fair. It won't matter if we don't have the locket; she'd still kill us for stealing from her."

Ryland shrugged. "Then I guess we're just going to have to get in and out of there without getting caught."

Venn gritted his teeth, his nostrils flaring. His skin rippled as if he was fighting the urge to shift.

"Maybe..." Fiona said cautiously. "Maybe Ryland's right. Maybe this is our only option."

"See?" Ryland pressed. "Even Fiona agrees with me."

Teagan sighed and shot Venn a somber expression. "I agree, too."

I would've put my vote in, but it would've been a selfish vote. And I was pretty sure my vote wasn't needed anyway.

Venn fumed, pressing his hands to his face and then raking his fingers through his hair. He took a long inhale and then let it all out in a *whoosh*. "I can't believe we're doing this. Fine. I will help you. I just hope you know what you're getting yourselves into."

Hope surged through my chest.

We're back in business!

15

Sneaking into a vampire nest in the dead of night should've scared the shit out of me. Instead, my heart pounded in exhilaration. This was way cooler than sitting on rooftops hoping to find trouble. This time, I was *causing* trouble. And I was pretty darn proud of it.

We waited until nightfall to crash the nest. Vampire nests were packed during the day since they were all sleeping to avoid the sunlight that burned their flesh. At night, vamps were either working or hanging out at bars or casinos, giving us the perfect opportunity to slip inside unnoticed.

According to Venn, most of Maliya's business took place inside the mansion, but the worst of her henchmen would be out "recruiting" blood slaves or making deals. The place wouldn't be completely empty, but there'd be significantly fewer vamps to risk running into. Plus, Venn guessed that we'd find the locket near the sleeping quarters, which would be virtually deserted by now.

How he knew so much about Maliya's mansion, I didn't

know. By the look Fiona shot me when I started to ask about it, I was pretty sure it was a story for another day.

We were all dressed in black, making us almost invisible against the night. The moon was high above us, casting a dull glow across the forest, just enough to make out the shadows of the trees. Ryland, Fiona, Venn, and I wove through the trees, careful not to make any noise. Teagan hadn't wanted to stay behind, despite the fact that she still looked like she needed rest, but Ryland insisted on it. He finally convinced her when he pointed out that her human heartbeat was enough to break our cover.

The mansion was tucked in the forest a half-mile off the road just outside of Nocton. The trees stopped at a brick wall surrounding the property.

"You're up, Rae," Ryland hissed through the darkness.

I didn't think Ryland trusted me, not when I agreed to play my part only if Venn helped me navigate the mansion after we retrieved the locket. Ryland was adamantly against that, saying he wouldn't let Venn hang back for me, but Venn insisted it was his own choice. Ryland finally caved, since I was their only hope of avoiding security cameras and alarms.

I jumped and shifted mid-air, grateful to be back in my own enchanted clothing. I flapped my wings until I was high enough to perch on the edge of the wall, which stood at least ten feet high. I already knew what the mansion would look like from the image I saw in the salt at Genevieve's, but that quick glance wasn't enough to truly prepare me for the beauty of the property.

I faced the West corner of the mansion, where the windows were dark. A vast garden surrounded by a manicured lawn stretched out toward the back of the property. It met up with perfectly trimmed bushes lining the side of the building. The front exterior was lit up like there were tiny little stars embedded into the brick. A long driveway circled the fountain near the main doors and seemed to go on forever before it reached a big iron gate by the road. The mansion itself was styled with white brick, and several towers with balconies reached up three stories. The building was divided into at least five different sections, each one bigger than the last. It seemed to go on for miles.

The property was quiet. Almost too quiet.

This is going to be a piece of cake.

Once I had a chance to take in the grandeur of the mansion, I turned to focusing on the smaller details. I spotted two security cameras hanging from the wall, pointing at the lawn. Another was secured next to the balcony doors looking over the garden. I scanned the area again, just to make sure, but it looked like I only had three security cameras to deal with.

I launched myself into the air and landed on the wall beside the first camera. I shifted back into human form and balanced myself on the edge of the wall above the camera. My feet dangled on either side of it. I grabbed the camera and twisted slowly, making sure not to make any sudden movements. I didn't want to catch anyone's eye if they were watching the security footage. The camera pivoted on its mount with ease. I pointed it toward the opposite end of the lawn and then shifted back into my raven form and did the same with the other two security cameras.

I glided over the top of the wall and circled around my co-conspirators. As soon as I cocked my head at them, they sprang into action. Ryland laced his fingers together and helped boost Venn over the wall. He landed quietly in the grass on the other side. Next, Fiona stepped into Ryland's hands, and she pulled herself over the wall. Venn helped her down on the other side.

Ryland backed up and took a running start. He launched himself upward and just barely caught the top of the wall with the ends of his fingers. He pulled himself up easily. Frankly, I was impressed. This guy must've been a champion at chin-ups. He jumped down from the wall and rolled onto the grass to slow his momentum.

Nobody spoke. Instead, we communicated through small hand gestures. Venn pointed to a balcony on the second level, and Ryland shot him a thumbs up. Then Venn gestured to one of the five chimneys. I nodded before he, Ryland, and Fiona hurried away from me across the lawn.

The plan was simple. I'd fly down the chimney to get inside undetected. Meanwhile, Venn, Ryland, and Fiona would climb the balcony. Once I reached the target room, I'd unlock the door from the inside to avoid triggering any alarms.

I flapped my wings and rose high above the mansion, my eyes fixed on the chimney. My heart pounded, partially because I feared what might be at the bottom of it—perhaps a room filled with hungry vampires—and partially from the thrill.

Bring on the vampires.

Without hesitation, I dove into the deep darkness. The chimney was cramped. It certainly wasn't wide enough to spread my wings. Despite clawing at the bricks to slow my fall, I spiraled downward, slamming into the sides and picking up mounds of soot as I went. I landed at the bottom in a pile of ash with a hard *thud.* The wind knocked out of me, but I ignored the burn in my chest as I righted myself, prepared for whatever might be waiting for me.

I was relieved to see that the room was empty. I stepped out onto a brick base that surrounded the fireplace. The room was dark, but I could make out shadows of bookcases and a long desk in the corner. It appeared as if I'd entered a study, which was exactly where Venn had told me I'd end up.

I shifted back to human form, ignoring the soot in my hair, and hurried to the door. I opened it a crack and peered down the hall. It was deserted.

Slowly, I pulled the door open and scurried down the hallway to the door on the end. It was open, revealing a long flight of stairs leading to the basement. I descended the stairs, my footsteps far too loud in the empty stairwell. At the bottom, a long, dark hallway stretched in front of me. The only light seeped in from an open door toward the end of the hall.

My heart pounded, and I welcomed the adrenaline. It'd be nice to get in at least one vampire ass-whooping tonight. Except for the part where Venn told me to avoid a fight unless absolutely necessary. And even then, he didn't want me killing any vamps. He said it'd only earn me a target on my back. Not like that was anything new, but I'd do my best to follow his instructions.

I inched forward, making sure my footsteps were soft as I passed door after door. I counted each door as I went, knowing I needed to pass three on the right before I reached my destination. I only crept closer to the door with the light on.

Finally, I reached out for the door I needed. Just as I twisted the knob, the door at the end of the hall swung open wider.

"Hey!" a deep voice shouted.

Instinct told me to spring into action, but instead I froze.

Plan B: If caught, just play the part. According to Venn, so many people milled around this place that most wouldn't give it a second thought, but they *would* come after you if you ran.

"What are you doing down here?" A huge guy emerged from the room and locked eyes with me. Even in the dim light, I could make out his pale skin and silver eyes.

I could totally take him. Maybe. Probably not. He was built like a bodybuilder.

"Laundry, sir," I lied, using my best submissive tone. I dropped my gaze to the guy's chest. Venn told me not to look the vamps straight in the eye.

Bodybuilder glared down at me disapprovingly. "Laundry runs during the day. You should know that."

"Sorry, sir," I said, improvising. "I'm new. I came in with the last group of blood slaves and was assigned to laundry duty. I just wanted to learn my way around."

"I thought they had a tour yesterday." Bodybuilder inhaled, as if searching for my scent. When he didn't find it, a smile crept across his face. He could tell I was a shifter, and he knew I'd make one heck of a meal.

"There were some reassignments," I lied. "I missed the first tour."

Bodybuilder stepped forward, gazing at me like he wanted to eat me. Which was probably true. "So, you haven't been assigned to anyone yet?"

I stepped back, still clinging on to my submissive act. "I thought you weren't supposed to feed off anyone but your own. Isn't Maliya strict about that?"

Bodybuilder scoffed. "She doesn't care unless you've already been assigned."

"I'm being assigned soon," I said. "I'll need my strength."

I loved how frightened I sounded. It was damn convincing.

"Assignments won't be for another week." Bodybuilder said, taking another step closer to me. "You'll regain your strength by then."

"Won't you lose your job?" I pulled at any strings I could. Not because I was scared, but because I didn't want this to get messy.

"I'll bring that up with Maliya myself," Bodybuilder snarled. "You should really learn to keep your mouth shut, shifter girl. You'll not want to *ever* forget your place here."

Bodybuilder lunged for me so fast that I didn't have time to react. His strong arm gripped my wrist, and his fangs elongated. I quickly calculated my options. On the one hand, I could play the part. On the other, this sure fell into the *absolutely necessary* category.

I'd already been bit once. And damn, it felt great. No one ever told me it would feel so good, like all the worries in the world didn't matter. If I'd let that vamp feed on me any longer, I might've never wanted him to stop. Maybe there was a reason blood slaves didn't run. It was like a drug. But I wasn't a druggie. No one got anywhere near my blood without my consent.

I swung my elbow upward. It connected with Bodybuilder's nose with a sickening *crunch*. His hands flew to his face. I didn't waste any time swinging my knee into his groin as hard as I could. He let out a grunt and sank to the ground, but not before reaching out and grabbing my arm, pulling me to the floor with inhuman strength. Pain shot across my shoulder as my body slammed into the ground. Bodybuilder jumped on top of me, his fangs heading straight for my neck.

I struggled against him, my breathing ragged. Maybe attacking was a bad move. A vamp of Cowen's size I could handle, but I didn't have the strength to combat this guy. He held my wrists against the ground and used his weight to keep my hips against the floor. It all happened so fast, and I mentally screamed at myself for letting him get me in this position. Rule one of fighting vampires: Don't ever let them get the upper hand. If you do, you're dead.

Shifter magic tingled through my body. My wrists shrank out of Bodybuilder's arms, and within a second, I was free. Bodybuilder nearly squashed me, but he caught himself. I managed to squeeze out from beneath his giant belly. I dove for him and slashed my talons across the top of his head. It was enough to make him pause, though he didn't cry out in pain as I expected him to. I was about to go for his eyes—always the eyes; those were the best part—when Bodybuilder's arm shot out and he scooped me out of the air.

For the first time all night, my heart pounded not from the excitement but from fear. Bodybuilder drew his arm back and whipped me against the wall. My small raven body slumped to the ground as I gasped for air, my back throbbing. Bodybuilder stood and stalked toward me, a triumphant smirk fixed to his face.

I didn't have time to catch my breath. If Bodybuilder got ahold of me, he was going to suck me two pints from dry. I was sure of it.

Not today, asshole!

He loomed over me and reached down. Before his hands could touch my feathers, I sprang out of his reach. Within a second, I was already shifting back into human form. Using all my strength, I jumped and kicked off the wall then spun mid-air, my leg aimed at his face. My heel cracked against the side of his head.

Bodybuilder's entire body flew sideways. His head

slammed into the wall, and he slumped to the ground, unconscious.

I gazed down at him for only a second, trying to decide if I should leave him, kill him, or hide the body. I didn't know how long I had before someone else came down here, so I didn't want to leave him. Venn made it clear I wasn't to kill anyone, so that was out of the question. *If we kill one of them, they'll come after us with an army*, he'd said. If I left him here, I only had to worry about one vamp with a vengeance. Which meant I had to hide him and hope he didn't wake up anytime soon.

I hooked my arms under his. With all my strength, I dragged the huge dude down the hall and dropped him into a storage closet.

A moment later, the sound of footsteps reached my ears. My whole body tensed, alert. Without another thought, I raced into the room I'd intended to enter earlier. It was so dark that I couldn't see. Instinctively, I ducked into the first hiding place I could find with my hands. Fabric brushed by my face as I crouched in a narrow cubby space. Curtains, maybe?

"Dave?" I heard a deep voice outside the room. "Where'd you go? I brought you a soda."

My guess was soda was code word for "fresh blood."

Footsteps continued down the hall, and then I heard the sound of a door swinging open. Every inch of my body tensed as the footsteps neared the room I hid in. I held my breath, and my fingers curled into fists. Maybe this whole thing was a bad idea. We should've just forgotten about the locket.

Retrieve the locket, and Venn will help you get to Cowen, I reminded myself.

The door swung open. I squeezed my eyes shut, like that might make me invisible.

Don't be scared, Rachel. Vampires don't scare you.

True. They didn't scare me... when I had a chance at escape. But here, my only chance at escape was the door I'd come through, the door a vampire was standing in right now.

"Dave?" the vampire called loud and clear.

I pictured him glancing around the dark room, but I didn't open my eyes to check. I just held my breath, feeling like my lungs might explode. Thank God I wasn't human. He'd hear my heart pounding for sure.

The door clicked shut, and I finally let my breath out. It felt like the first breath I'd taken in the last five minutes. Slowly, I emerged from my hiding spot.

My eyes finally adjusted to the darkness. A small window set high in the wall let in a small amount of light. I noticed several large appliances lining the far wall. When I glanced back to where I'd been hiding, I realized I'd been behind a row of clothes hanging off a closet rod. I'd known I was headed for the laundry room, but I pictured a small room with one washer and dryer, not a huge room fit for a resort. Then again, I suppose they needed it when they had a house the size of a hotel.

I crossed the room and stopped when I reached the opposite wall. Just inches above my head, a square tube came down from the ceiling.

Bet they thought their laundry chute was safe. They should know better than that.

I shifted into raven form and flew up to the laundry chute, wedging myself in. Like the chimney, it wasn't large enough for me to spread my wings in, but I was able to wiggle my way up by digging my talons into the wood on one side and pressing my back against the other.

The chute was cramped and stuffy, and I swore I only moved an inch a minute, but eventually, I reached the top. I kicked at the door, and it popped open. It took a crazy ninja move to launch myself out of the chute without falling all the way back down. Somehow, I managed to rustle my way out, though a couple of my feathers were now crooked.

I shifted and glanced around the room bathed in darkness. It was vast, with doors heading off in all directions. I guessed one of them had to be the bathroom, and another a closet. The two double doors must've led out into the hall.

A king bed stood at the center of the room, with a plush chasse situated at the end of it, and a chandelier hung from the tall ceiling. A long line of windows lined one wall, all covered in dark black curtains that had been pulled aside to offer a view of the garden.

Voices in the hall reached my ears, sending another surge of adrenaline through my veins. Getting caught was *not* part of the plan. I wouldn't be able to talk my way out of what I was doing in Maliya's bedroom. I scurried under the bed and tried to control my breathing, but it was shallow and ragged. I covered my mouth to keep from making any kind of noise.

To my relief, the voices continued down the hall. I still waited at least another minute before I crawled out from under the bed and got to my feet. I rushed over to the glass doors leading onto the balcony and twisted the lock. Ryland, Fiona, and Venn hurried over from where they hid in the shadows when I opened the door.

Venn's hands were on the side of my face immediately, his eyes roaming mine for sign of injury. When he didn't spot any in the darkness, he pulled me into a hug, sending my heart pounding so quickly that I was sure he could feel it. His breath rushed across my face, and my chest pressed against his. My whole body warmed in his arms. He held on to me protectively, and for a moment, I truly felt safe in his arms—albeit at risk of a heart attack.

This was the perfect time to make some snarky comment about how he could at least take me on a date first, but I held my tongue. I rather preferred the comforting embrace.

"Thank God," Venn whispered. "We thought you'd been caught."

"What took you so long?" Ryland hissed.

"I fell in," I deadpanned.

"What?" He looked completely confused.

I shook my head as I drew away from Venn. "Never mind. Let's find that locket."

We all split off in different directions. I headed straight for the jewelry on the vanity across the room, Fiona silently opened drawers on a dresser nearby, and Ryland felt around on the bed.

Because she's totally keeping it under her sheets. It's not a freaking diary.

"Over here," Venn whispered. He cocked his finger for us to follow him.

Venn led us over to a door with a keypad above the knob. He took a deep breath.

"How can he know the combination?" I whispered to Fiona.

She just gave me a shrug, but something told me she knew exactly how. Venn knew *way* too much about this mansion, about Maliya. It wasn't hard to figure out why, but I didn't want to believe it. And that wasn't exactly the kind of thing you just brought up in casual conversation.

The keypad beeped twice. Victory surged through me, but the feeling didn't last long. Venn cursed under his breath. My face fell. Those weren't the beeps of a successful combination. It was an error message.

"I thought you knew the passcode," Ryland whispered.

"I did." Venn scowled at him. "But I also told you it could've changed. There was more than one reason I didn't want to go through with this plan."

"So we can't get in?" Ryland sounded less than pleased.

I was feeling pretty much the same way. This plan was never going to work in our favor. How could I have thought it would?

"I get three tries. Let me try something else." Venn placed his fingers at the corner of his eyes, like he was thinking really hard.

Seconds ticked by. The room was eerily silent apart from everyone's breathing. I was half considering jumping forward and entering a random combination myself—even though there were probably a million combinations.

Finally, Venn opened his eyes and input a four-digit code. To my surprise, the lock disengaged. Venn twisted the knob, and the door swung open. When Venn said we'd have to break in to Maliya's vault, I pictured a bank vault with safety deposit boxes or something. I didn't picture a freaking room full of treasure.

Soft lighting illuminated the room when we stepped inside. It was the size of a large walk-in closet, with display cases lining the walls. Expensive jewelry sparkled beneath the glass. When I said expensive, I meant *expensive*. Like, probably in the millions. There was even a tiara placed in the center of the display case on the left, embedded with hundreds of shining diamonds. It wasn't just jewelry, either. I spotted a knife and an old coin, too. I wasn't sure of the significance of it all, but everything either looked old or worth a fortune. It took my breath away.

"Be quick," Venn warned.

I stepped further into the room, searching for any sign of a locket. My heart leapt in my chest when the door beeped. I whirled around. We all exchanged a quick, alarmed expression, but it only lasted a split second. The door began swinging shut on its own.

"Run!" Ryland commanded the same time Fiona cursed under her breath.

Everyone sprang toward the moving door at the same time. Ryland made it out first, followed by Venn. I sprinted behind Fiona. Just before I made it to the door, my eyes caught sight of a golden locket in one of the display cases. I didn't think twice of my next move. I reached for the glass and flipped the top up. I snatched the locket out of the case.

Fiona cried out in pain. The door had caught her on her way out, pinning her shoulder to the frame. There was no way I was fitting through the opening behind her. I shifted in a flash and scooped up the locket in my beak. Fiona managed to wiggle herself free, no doubt thanks to someone on the other side tugging at her.

I didn't question my chances. I jumped for the crack in the door. The edge of the door brushed by my feathers. I thought for sure it would squash me and cut my head off or something, but by some miracle, I slipped out of the door with my head still intact.

Venn had stopped in the middle of the room and was ushering everyone toward the balcony. Fiona held on to her shoulder and sprinted behind Ryland. Venn's eyes met mine, and I spread my wings. Venn took it as a cue to whirl around and follow behind everyone else. He knew I was right behind him.

We did it!

I couldn't believe it.

Doors banged open behind me. I didn't have time to react before something wrapped tightly around my leg and dragged me out of the air.

I spoke too soon.

The blood drained from my face as my eyes connected with Venn's. Horror washed over his expression, but he'd already taken the leap over the balcony. His hands reached out, desperate to grab on to anything to come back for me, but his body betrayed him. Within a mere split second, he was gone.

Somebody grabbed me by the back of the neck so hard I couldn't move. I feared whoever had ahold of me might crush the vertebra in my neck if I did. Strong hands lifted my raven form until I dangled several feet off the ground. My vision began to blur due to lack of blood flow, but I saw enough to count at least five male vampires surrounding me. One of them rushed past me and leapt from the balcony, pursuing my friends.

And then a woman's voice reached my ears. A thin figure with wide hips that swayed with each step entered through the double doors. "What do we have here, boys?"

Maliya.

I swallowed deeply and locked my jaw tight. The necklace hung from my beak.

Never let a vampire get the upper hand, I repeated. *If you do, you're dead.*

I didn't know what would happen next, but one thing was for certain: No matter what, I was already dead.

16

I had a rule about death. If I ever faced it, I was fighting back until my last breath.

My eyes darted to the lamp on the bedside table mere feet from me. Within a split second, I shifted. My hand shot out and clamped around the lamp, and I swung it above my head with as much force as I could. It slammed into the vampire's head behind me and snapped at the base.

Big Bad Vamp released his hold on me just enough that I was able to duck and spin out of his grasp. I sprinted for the balcony doors, but a shadow leapt in front of me. All I saw was orange hair glistening in the moonlight before strong hands slammed into my chest, sending me flying backward across the room. I landed on the bed, bouncing across the mattress as all the wind left my chest.

Before I had a chance to process what had just happened, another vamp with dark hair and a square jaw was already on top of me, reaching out for the locket hanging from my mouth. One hand pressed down hard on my throat while the other pulled at the necklace. I bit down on the chain as my fingers reached for the other bedside table, blindly searching for another weapon. My left hand curled around something cool and hard. I swung it toward the vamp's head.

Before it could connect with his skull, the ginger guy leapt onto the bed. His hand shot out of the darkness and grabbed my wrist. He threw my arm sideways with such force that I couldn't control my own body's momentum. The object in my hand crashed into the edge of the table, and the sound of breaking glass met my ears. Cool water rushed over my hand, and I realized it was a vase.

Ginger plunged his fingers into my hair and wrenched the strands backward as he squeezed my lower jaw, trying to force my teeth apart. I refused, welcoming the fire across my skull and the intense pressure on my jaw more than I welcomed failure.

My fingers tightened around the broken vase. With all my strength, I thrust it upward. The sharp, ragged edges sank into Ginger's chest. In an instant, his hands in my hair and on my jaw disappeared. Ash rained down on me.

Square Jaw's eyes darted momentarily to where his friend had just been. It was enough of a distraction that I was able to swipe his hand off my throat. I thrust my hips upward, spinning our bodies until I had him pinned down on the bed.

A look of desire crossed his eyes, and he opened his mouth. But he didn't even get a chance to take a breath before the shards of glass in my hand entered his heart. I didn't stick around to enjoy his body disintegrating to ash. I leapt off the bed and shifted, aiming for the balcony doors. The locket still hung in my beak.

Without warning, my skull slammed into a solid, invisible barrier. My neck twisted, and pain jolted through it as the ligaments twisted. I fell to the ground in a daze. The room swam around me as a strong hand reached out and curled around the back of my neck. Big Bad Vamp squeezed tightly. I swore he was a second away from snapping my neck. It freaking *hurt*.

Maliya only laughed and stepped forward. Her long dark hair swayed around her. She snatched the locket out of my beak. Though I tried to hold on, it slipped through my grasp.

"Shift," she commanded in an unforgiving tone.

I hesitated. I didn't take well to those types of demands.

The hold on my neck tightened again. I did as I was told. My body lengthened, and my wings grew into arms. My nostrils flared. Almost immediately, Maliya's hand cracked across the side of my face. Pain pulsed across my skin, but I didn't make a sound.

Maliya leaned in close to me. She stood several inches higher, but I guessed she was wearing heels under her dark red dress. "How *dare* you," she hissed, sounding strangely reminiscent of a snake. "How dare you steal from me!"

My captor hurled me across the floor, his fingers leaving my neck as I flew through the air. I landed with a *thud* and skidded across the carpet past Maliya and straight between the double doors leading to the hall. I was already dizzy from the earlier impact, but my headache intensified at the sudden movement. I glanced toward the balcony and finally saw what I had missed a moment ago. The doors were shut, the glass blocking my only chance of escape.

A vampire by the doors—the one who'd shut them, I assumed—stepped forward. *Cowen.* He had a look of fury etched into his eyes. There was no doubt in my mind that he recognized me.

Maliya knelt to my level, fuming. "Who sent you? Who are

the other people you were with, and how did you manage to get the passcode to my vault?"

I held my tongue. I may be going down, but I wasn't taking Venn and the rest of them with me. They'd been nothing but nice to me. It was almost a glimpse into the family I once had, before the vampires stole them from me.

Shock riveted through me when Maliya grabbed me by the shirt and hauled me to my feet. I stumbled backward, and she slammed me into the wall.

In the hallway light, I finally got a good look at her. She was flawlessly beautiful, with long dark lashes, high cheek bones, and manicured eyebrows. Her skin was pale, but not as pale as the other vampires, as if her skin had a darker hue during her time as a human. Her black hair fell in perfect waves around her shoulders. Her long-sleeved dress gave her breasts the perfect lift—to the point where I was a little jealous. She looked like she might be in her forties, and *my* breasts weren't even that perky. Everything about her screamed *cougar*, though there were the obvious silver eyes and elongated fangs that said *vampire*. Who knew, though? She could be a vampire cougar. Probably was.

Maliya's snarl turned into a sardonic smile. "Don't want to talk?" she taunted. "Fine with me. It's not going to save your sorry shifter ass anyway."

This bitch has no right to talk to me like that!

My head snapped forward, cracking into hers. Her head reeled backward, but it barely looked like she felt a thing. Meanwhile, my head and neck throbbed. Big Bad Vamp stepped forward, but she held up a hand to stop him before he could get to me. I was probably more shocked than anyone. I hadn't planned on head-butting her.

Maliya's silver eyes slowly roamed over me. "I've been

looking for you for a long time, *raven shifter*. How fortunate that you just happened to find me on your own."

Looking for me? Great. Who'd I kill?

"You *are* the Ravenite, aren't you?" Maliya accused in a smooth, even tone.

Ugh. That name again.

I didn't even bother responding. I wouldn't play into her games.

"Will you kill her?" Cowen asked.

I'd kill all these jackasses first.

A smile spread across Maliya's face, but she didn't tear her gaze off mine. "No. That would be too easy. I want the Ravenite to *suffer*."

What had I gotten myself into?

Maliya dropped her grip on my shirt and whirled around. She unclasped the locket in her hand and secured it around her neck, placing it over several other necklaces that hung there. "Lock her up. Don't provide her any food or water. I'll be back to deal with her later."

Big Bad Vamp grabbed on to both of my arms as Maliya headed down the hall with Cowen at her heels. I kicked my legs into the air, trying to struggle out of his grasp, but he was too strong. He squeezed my arms together behind my back until I thought my shoulders might pop out of their sockets.

"What'd I do to you?" I blurted. I hadn't intended to speak, but for the life of me, I couldn't figure out what I'd done to get her attention. I mean, besides try to steal from her and head-butt her in the face. But she spoke of me—of the Ravenite— like she already had something against me long before tonight. "Did I kill one of your security guards or something?"

That was very possible. I'd killed a lot of vampires. I couldn't exactly keep track.

Maliya spun toward me and was back in front of me in an instant, her breath rushing across my face. "No," she snarled. "You killed my *husband*."

Every muscle in my body froze at her words. I really had gotten myself in too deep. Whatever torture she had in store for me, it wasn't going to be pretty.

And still, I couldn't seem to bite my tongue. The next words slipped out without my approval. "I'm sure he deserved it."

Big. Mistake.

A scream ripped out of my lungs and echoed down the hall when Maliya's fangs sank into my neck and a shock of vampire venom entered my veins.

17

Excruciating pain seared through my body. I could hardly focus on my limbs, let alone my own thoughts. Each time my consciousness broke through the pain, I racked my brain trying to decide if there was a stronger word than *bitch* to describe Maliya. I'd run into my fair share of bitches in my lifetime. I survived high school, after all. But *bitch* was such a petty little word. Maliya was pure evil.

She barely bit me for a second. It was hardly deep enough to bleed and wasn't long enough to change me—just enough to make me suffer. She knew exactly how much venom would keep me just on the edge of consciousness so that I could feel every nerve ending in my body ablaze. It started at my skin, the hot, widespread pain of being cast into the fires of Hell. Then it moved to my muscles, where the pain transformed into sharp, repetitive jabs. It was like being stabbed over and over again with long surgical needles on every inch of my body. And then it reached my bones, where it felt as if someone was cutting them open with a chainsaw and shoving metal rods through them.

I almost wished the pain meant something, like I'd come out on the other side of it with flawless beauty and immortality. But I'd rather die than join the ranks of the most hated and heartless species alive. Still, immortality beat this fiery pain burning through my veins.

It seemed like days that I'd been stuck inside my own head, trying to claw my way through agony. Eventually, the pain eased to a dull ache, and my mind cleared enough that I managed to force my eyes open.

The first thing I noticed was a charge like electricity buzzing through the air. I was in a small room no bigger than my bathroom, lying on a stone floor with identical walls on three sides of me. A layer of bars blocked me from a larger room that spanned beyond my cell.

I lifted my head, which was still foggy from the venom, and squinted into the darkness. There wasn't much of a room outside my cell. It was more like a hallway, with at least a dozen other cells identical to mine lining the walls on either side. A soft light cast shadows across the room. When my eyes finally focused, I saw that the light came from a single candle near a large metal door. A vampire sat in a wooden chair next to it.

A guard.

His eyes were closed, like he didn't take his job seriously. I couldn't help but think that the stone cells and candlelight were all there for show, just to give me the creeps. I mean, who had a freaking *dungeon* in their house?

I had to remind myself that Maliya literally had blood *slaves* living here. This was probably where they went to get punished.

I pushed myself to my elbows, but I could barely make my muscles comply to my demands. This was a thousand times worse than last time. It was less like I was recovering from a marathon and more like I was a cadaver waking from the morgue.

My tongue felt like sandpaper. I tried to lick my lips, but there was nothing left to wet them with. They were dry and cracked, like my throat. My stomach twisted in hunger. I didn't know how long I'd been here.

My thoughts flickered to Venn, the look in his eyes when he realized I'd been caught and that he couldn't save me. I wanted to believe he'd come for me, but it didn't matter how much he knew about this mansion. There was no way he was getting down in this dungeon—past Maliya, who now had the power to predict the future, past the security cameras, and past the guard at the end of the hall. I wouldn't be surprised if there was another guard posted outside the door.

Not to mention that I was pretty sure Ryland would talk anyone out of coming back for me. I mean, he wasn't a terrible person or anything, but he seemed like the kind of guy who wouldn't risk his family for a girl he just met. I wished I could believe Venn would defy Ryland's instructions and come after me like a true knight in shining armor, but I wasn't holding my breath.

Which meant I was on my own. I'd shift, slip through the bars, attack the guard, and figure out the rest as I went. It was a long shot considering my whole body trembled in weakness, but I held on to my slim chance of survival.

Shifter magic tingled across my skin. As quickly as it came, it disappeared. What the hell? I tried again, but it was like trying to run through a brick wall. My skin rippled, but the change never happened. Was it the vampire venom? No. That shouldn't affect shifter magic.

I tried again. The strange buzzing I sensed intensified as if pushing back against my magic. Terror consumed me when I realized the energy in the air was a strong enchantment keeping me from shifting. Strange. I'd never felt someone else's magic before. I'd heard it was possible, but I'd never been strong enough to recognize it.

Hopelessness consumed me, sinking like a rock in my gut. I curled my knees to my chest as every curse word I knew flew through my mind. I screwed up *big* time. I should've gone after Jenna sooner. I shouldn't have begged Venn for help. I should've let the vamps take the locket so I could escape. I should've fought harder. I should've done a lot of things... Then I wouldn't be in this mess.

Who was I kidding? This was where my search for Jenna was always going to end. I was actively pursuing the Soulless, which meant I was going to die at the hands of a vamp one way or another. It was kind of in the job description.

I pushed the unkind words I had for myself from my head. My mind drifted to a simpler time. I was seven, pumping my legs on the swings at the park near our house, trying to swing higher than Jenna.

I was eight, running through the sprinkler in our back yard on a hot summer day while Jenna chased me around with a pool noodle.

I was ten, sitting in front of the mirror in Jenna's room while she dusted blush on my face and nearly impaled me in the eye with a mascara brush.

I was twelve, sneaking out to the treehouse after bedtime to meet up with Jenna and "practice magic." Mom and Dad didn't approve of magic, so mine and my sister's curiosity had to go under the radar. We didn't know then that I was a witch.

My head snapped upward as it hit me. What was I *doing*? I was a witch. I could get out of this place on my own. I mean, I didn't know a spell to unlock jail cells or anything, but I was desperate. Maybe that was enough to save my life...

I tried not to make any sudden movements so that the guard wouldn't notice. First things first—get rid of the guard. I was too weak to take him one-on-one.

Slowly, I rose to my feet. My whole body tensed with nerves. There was nowhere in the cell to rest my shivering body, not even a cot to sit down on. So I stood there with my knees quivering and my hands curled into tight fists. I narrowed my eyes at the sleeping guard, focusing intently on aiming my magic at him like a laser beam. Maybe if I concentrated hard enough, he'd have a heart attack or burst into flame or something.

Several minutes passed, and... it was incredibly anticlimactic. The guard didn't move, and all my concentration did was give me a headache.

So maybe I couldn't make vampires spontaneously combust. Instead, I turned my attention to the lock on my cell. It was my only other option. I didn't know the incantation to unlock a door—I'd never needed it before—but it couldn't be that hard. I was sure any low witch was capable of it.

I stepped forward and reached out until my hands closed around the cold metal of the lock. I pictured the locking mechanism disengaging and the door swinging open, but when I pushed at the cell door, it remained firmly in place.

"Come on," I growled under my breath. *I can do this.*

The tension in my head intensified. Okay, so maybe it wouldn't work with all this negative energy pulsing through me. Freaking Synchrony. How was I supposed to channel positive energy in my situation?

Just try it.

I closed my eyes and took a deep breath, forcing out the tension in my head. But all it did was transfer that tension to my shoulders. I tried again.

This has to work.

I pushed at my cell door again. It didn't budge. My jaw tightened, and I resisted the urge to kick the metal bars.

This is dumb! I bet Synchrony isn't even real. It's the freaking enchantment working against me.

The sound of a lock slipping open echoed through the dungeon. It startled the guard awake and sent me stumbling backward into the far wall of my cell.

"This shouldn't take long, Cowen," I heard a female voice say on the other side of the door. "You'll have plenty of time to make your flight to Seattle. You can tell Ellwood all about the raven bitch once you get there."

Seconds later, the door at the end of the hall burst open. Maliya entered the dungeon, flanked by four male vampires. Through the darkness, I recognized Cowen, Bodybuilder, and Big Bad Vamp beside her. The other guy was new. Maliya's heels clicked against the stone in a quick staccato that matched the pace of my pounding heart.

I am not afraid, I told myself, despite every biological process assuring me I was. I ignored the warnings my own body was giving me and straightened in my cell. My eyes locked on Maliya's, and my face softened into a perfectly indifferent expression. The sound of her footsteps stopped once she was within arm's distance of my cell. I could've reached through the bars and clawed at her face.

"Let her out, Dave," Maliya commanded in a cold tone. She never broke eye contact with me.

Dave—a.k.a. Bodybuilder—stepped forward. He glared at me with a hard expression. No doubt it was more than a little embarrassing that a huge vampire like him lost a fight to a little girl. I expected him to whisper some sort of threat, but he didn't speak. He simply unlocked my cell and stepped aside.

"Get her," Maliya instructed before turning her back to me.

Dave reached into the cell. Though I ducked out of the way on instinct, he had me in his hands in under a second. His grip was so tight on my arms that I was sure he'd leave hand-shaped bruises behind. I stumbled out of my cell, a thousand curses thick on the end of my tongue. I didn't speak. I didn't need to add fuel to the fire, though I would very much enjoy seeing how that would go down.

"Bring it in, Vincent," Maliya called to the guard.

Dave hauled me down the long hallway, even though he didn't have to. I would've walked on my own if he let me, but the more I struggled to regain my footing, the more he fought against me.

The guard appeared in the doorway, dragging a chair behind him. It was the size of my dad's old plushy recliner, only it was made entirely of wood. Two of the legs screeched across the stone floor, and the other two connected with the ground with a loud *thud* when he dropped it into place at the end of the line of cells.

I spotted the shackles connected to the arms and legs of the chair, and that's when I freaked out. My legs thrashed, and my arms flailed. My elbow caught Dave in the nose. Two of the other vampires reached for me and held my legs. Maliya just stood there with a smirk on her face, watching her henchmen force me into the chair.

"Get off me!" I screamed.

Of course, they all ignored me. The cool metal of the

shackles touched my skin, and I heard the sound of them locking. I continued to struggle, though it was clearly no use. An icy cold hand shot out and grabbed my face, squeezing my cheeks until my teeth hurt.

"Stop!" Maliya demanded of me.

Despite the urge to spit in her face, I did as I was told. If I complied, maybe she'd have a little mercy on me.

She's a vampire, I reminded myself. *They have no mercy.*

"This entire room is enchanted," she warned. "Don't even think about shifting. It won't help you get free."

Maliya dropped her hand from my face, but she leaned in so close that I could smell the copper on her breath. I noticed the locket hanging from her neck. The candlelight near the door cast dancing shadows across her face. I pressed my head against the back of the chair, trying to get as far away from her as possible.

"Ivan Valerik," she whispered, accenting each syllable.

Huh? Was that some sort of incantation?

"Say his name," she instructed.

I kept my mouth shut.

Her palm cracked across the side of my face. My cheek stung, but after the pain I'd endured with her vampire venom, I barely felt it.

"Say. His. Name!" she shouted. "Ivan. Valerik!"

"Go to hell." The words slipped out before I could stop myself. But damn, they felt good.

Maliya plunged her hand into my hair and yanked back until my face tilted upward to look into her eyes. Her hold was so tight that I thought she might pull my hair out.

"It's not that hard!" she roared. "Say his name. Ivan Valerik."

It wasn't hard, but it sure gave me pleasure watching her

lips continue to tighten. I told myself I should just comply, but my mouth wouldn't move. My stubbornness could be a curse sometimes.

"You killed him!" she growled, pulling even harder on my hair.

"I don't remember an Ivan," I said in a completely calm and collected tone. Boy, did Maliya squirm. She didn't like it one bit that I wasn't crying out and begging for mercy. I sure loved toying with vampires. Might as well get one final game in.

"You're lying," Maliya accused.

She dropped my hair, though a dull ache continued to pulse where she'd been tugging at the strands. She stepped back a foot and held her hand out to Cowen. The bastard pulled a dagger from a sheath on his boot and handed it to her.

Maliya held the blade to my neck. It took everything I had not to blink, though my breathing was ragged. Instinct told me to fight back, to survive, but I didn't see a scenario where I made it out of here alive.

"I know you remember Ivan," Maliya insisted.

"I've killed a lot of vampires."

"Yes," Maliya agreed, "but you'd remember Ivan."

"Why's that?" I asked.

"Because," Maliya said, tightening her grip on the blade. "He was your first kill."

18

A sharp breath passed by my lips as the images of that night came flooding back. It was just over a year ago, a few months after I filed for emancipation, left my foster family, and moved to the city. I'd been plagued by insomnia and nightmares ever since my parents were killed. I'd stepped out onto my fire escape that night to get some fresh air since I couldn't sleep.

My chest tightened when I thought back to what I'd seen.

A woman's scream cut through the silence on the deserted street below me. My fingers tightened around the railing as I looked over the edge of the fire escape three stories down. Below, a man had cornered a woman in an alleyway across the street.

He's going to rape her, I thought immediately. I'd already lived through my parents' deaths and my sister's abduction. I couldn't take witnessing another act of violence.

"Please!" the woman begged, but the man continued to advance on her like a predator stalking his prey.

I couldn't let this happen. I shifted into raven form. It wasn't the first time I'd shifted, but I hadn't had many opportunities to fly—since I didn't want anyone knowing what I was. As I spread my wings and jumped off the fire escape, I found that flight came naturally to me.

I dove into the alleyway and tore a chunk of skin from the man's hand just moments before he touched the girl. He pulled away from her, holding on to his hand and cursing. I didn't see his silver eyes until I soared in a loop, preparing for my second attack.

My body should've been pulsing in terror, but my fear was pushed down by something else, by another internal instinct that told me to protect, to save. There wasn't time for fear.

Somehow, the silver eyes didn't intimidate me. He—Ivan—must've thought they should, because when I landed and shifted back into human form, he only laughed. Here I was, a seventeen-year-old girl who was half his size and butt naked, thinking I could take him on. He drastically underestimated me.

"Leave her alone," I demanded.

Ivan smirked, ignoring the girl he'd been stalking. Instead, he advanced on me. "A shifter?" he said suggestively. "You'll be worth quite a bit."

He lunged forward. I saw it coming and ducked out of the way, but he was too fast for me. He wrapped his arms around my chest. One hand assaulted my exposed breast while the other squeezed so tight I thought my ribs might crack. I cried out in pain, then dipped my head and bit down as hard as I could on his arm.

He growled and whipped my body around, flinging me across the alley. I skidded across the pavement. Tiny little pebbles and bits of dirt ripped through skin. Adrenaline shot through my body, and hot breath passed by my upper lip as he advanced. Bitch, I was only getting started.

I sprang to my feet. "Touch me again, and you'll regret it."

Ivan only smiled, as if he was amused by our little game. "Is that an invitation, shifter?"

"Hell no!" I jumped forward to attack, but he was already moving.

His fist connected with my gut, sending me reeling backward. My spine slammed into the nearby dumpster. I reached for the edge of it to catch myself, but my hand slipped inside. A jagged piece of metal at the top of the trash pile sliced across my palm. I inhaled a sharp breath and held my wounded hand in my good hand. Ivan's eyes darted to the blood dripping onto the pavement.

He licked his lips. "I always did like playing with my food."

"Too bad your mother never taught you manners."

Ivan leapt forward, his fangs bared for my bleeding hand. I didn't think; I only acted. I snatched up the scrap metal and aimed for his heart.

It cut into his chest like a knife through butter. A moment of shock crossed his face before his body disintegrated into a pile of ash. His clothes crumbled into a heap where he'd stood only a moment before.

For the first time in a year, I actually felt something more than misery. For a second, I wasn't suffering, because no matter how much anguish had come into my life recently, I could still do good in the world. I could still make a difference. I could save people from evil, keep them from suffering the way I had since the vampires stole something from me.

The woman I'd been protecting was already long gone, but I felt like she would've thanked me if she could.

I returned to my apartment that night never knowing I'd left a raven feather behind, not until the news reports came out the next day. As time went on, I got smarter about my attacks, but I always left a raven feather. That way, the vampires would know there was someone out there protecting Nocton.

That way, they knew to be afraid.

They named me the Raven of the Night, but a misprint from an online new source led to the shortened version—Ravenite. They'd called me that ever since. They hadn't really gotten my personality down, though, always calling me a vigilante and saying I was greater than I really was. One blog claimed I was as strong as ten male vampires put together, and one theorized that I must've been a vampire-shifter hybrid.

I'd managed to get away with it due to not being registered as a shifter and killing every vampire who saw me shift. I'd worried for months that the girl from that first night would turn me in, but she never did.

I didn't intend to become a vigilante. I just wanted to protect people...

Because I couldn't protect Jenna.

"Say. His. Name," Maliya repeated, pulling me back to the present.

I wouldn't. He didn't deserve to be acknowledged, not after what he would've done to that girl in the alley. I realized now he wasn't trying to rape her, but kidnapping her for the blood slave trade wasn't any better.

"All I want is for you to acknowledge that you killed him," Maliya said. "So, let's try this again."

Maliya slowly brought the blade between her lips and ran the dagger gently across her teeth. In a flash, she swung the dagger downward. The blade cut across my left forearm, sending vampire venom into my bloodstream. Fire ignited across my arm, burning down to my fingers and up my shoulder. Blood flowed out of the wound and crept down my arm. I shrieked like banshee, my scream echoing off the stone walls. The guard, Vincent, covered his hears with the heels of his hands and cursed.

"Say it!" Maliya demanded.

She sliced at my skin again, just above the last cut. It felt as if the blood in my arm had been replaced with hot lava. It compounded with the ache of venom that had saturated my body down to the bones last night. It was like Maliya's blade was skinning me alive, like the skin was ripping from the muscle and everything. It was unbearable. *Effing bitch.*

I just wanted the pain to stop.

"Ivan!" I cried before I consciously decided to give in. The name came out so high-pitched that it hardly sounded like a name at all.

"Again!" Maliya commanded as she slashed the blade across my skin a third time.

"Ivan!" I repeated. The words fell from my lips against my command as my self-preservation instinct kicked in. "Ivan Valerik."

Maliya paused with the blade at my skin, ready to make a fourth cut above the other three. I held my breath, forcing back the sobs bubbling up in my throat.

"There we go," she said happily. "Now, why couldn't you do that in the first place?"

My head hung in defeat, but I didn't respond. Beneath my waterfall of dark hair, my jaw clenched, and my nostrils flared.

Maliya held her head high. "I want you to admit what you did. You remember killing him, don't you?"

My hands shook, and though the shackles dug into my skin, I clenched my hands into fists. Every muscle in my body tightened, the tension most intense in my lips and eyebrows. Blood dripped from my arm and onto the floor.

Slowly, I lifted my head. "Yeah," I answered in a clipped tone. "I remember killing him. I remember everything."

My tone shifted, becoming light as air… almost dream-like. I knew it would piss Maliya off, and I loved to watch her squirm. "I remember the way the metal fragment cut through his chest. I'll never forget the look in his eyes when he realized me, a tiny little raven shifter, defeated him. I mean, he was *Ivan Valerik*, and mine was the last face he saw before he died. Before he was reduced to nothing more than a pile of ash at my feet—"

Maliya's hand shot out and clamped around my throat. She squeezed so tight I couldn't breathe. My eyes rolled back, and I gasped for breath that didn't come. I was pretty sure she was two seconds away from collapsing my trachea.

A *thud* sounded beside me, and then a grunt. Maliya's grip on my throat loosened momentarily. My eyes shot open just in time to see Dave's body crumble into a pile of ash beside Maliya. A knife clinkered to the ground atop his clothes.

As soon as that knife entered Dave's chest, hope entered mine. Teagan had made it, and she'd come with a message.

Today wasn't the day I'd die.

19

A low growl echoed down the hall and into the dungeon. *Venn*.

He'd come to save me. I could hardly believe it. And yet... I couldn't believe I ever doubted him.

"Get them!" Maliya shouted.

My back was to the door, and the chair I sat in was too big for me to peek around it, so I couldn't see what was going on. Three of Maliya's men disappeared from view to pursue my rescuers.

The growl behind me turned into a full-on howl. A breeze passed through my hair as a massive shadow leapt over my chair. In wolf form, Venn slammed into Maliya and knocked her flat on her back. I could hear the shuffling of bodies and the shouts that came from Maliya's men. Fiona's *yip* and Ryland's roar met my ears.

They were all here. For me. I was so happy I could cry.

Maliya held her hands over Venn's throat. His jaws snapped at her face, but she held him far enough away that he couldn't cause any damage. Maliya's fist swung upward and connected with the underside of his jaw. He let out a pained bark.

"Venn!" I cried in a shaky voice. I struggled against my restraints, but even my shifter strength wasn't enough to release me from the shackles.

Maliya lifted her knee and got her foot under him. She used all her leverage to hurl him off of her. He flew through the air faster than I could blink. His body crashed against one of the cage doors so violently that it made me wince. The door clanged loudly, masking his whimper of pain. My whole body ached for him.

"No!" I shrieked. It was horrifying to watch it happen without being able to help.

Venn slumped to the ground. He blinked rapidly, disoriented.

Maliya stood with a smirk on her face. "Venn," she said in mock disappointment. "I should've known it was you. Who else could've guessed the code to my vault?"

Venn finally got to his feet, but his chest heaved shallow breaths. He looked weak, like the blow to the bars had broken a rib or two. I wanted to rush over to him and heal him, but I couldn't move.

Maliya stalked forward. I expected her to kick Venn, but before she could, a small figure with red fur darted between her legs. Maliya tripped over Fiona in the most un-graceful way I'd ever seen. It was so satisfying to watch that I almost burst out laughing.

While Fiona had Maliya temporarily distracted, Venn shifted and rushed over to me.

"Are you okay?" he asked with worry in his eyes. He pushed my hair out of my face, and then his gaze fell to the gashes across my arm. I didn't have time to explain or to tell him how it felt like I'd reached my arm into the fires of hell.

"There!" I cocked my head toward the pile of clothes next to me.

Venn rifled through it and quickly found Dave's keys in the pants pocket. It took him a moment of shuffling through them to find one that resembled the right shape for the shackles. He shoved the key in the lock at my feet and twisted. I barely noticed the pressure on my ankles disappear; I couldn't feel much of anything outside of the sting shooting up and down my arm.

As soon as my hands were free, I jumped out of the chair and flung my arms around Venn's neck. I didn't even stop to think about what I was doing. I pressed my entire body to his and lifted my lips to meet his.

It was only meant to be a peck, a thank-you for rescuing me from Maliya's torture, but the moment our lips connected, time altogether seemed to stop. The grunts and screams around me faded, and it felt as if the floor fell away beneath our feet. Even the pain in my arm seemed to numb to nothing.

Venn wrapped his arms around me and squeezed me tight, like he wasn't at all surprised by the kiss, like he welcomed it, *craved* it even. My heart flipped in my chest. But it wasn't just a little flutter, like the tummy tickle you get when you drive over a hill too fast. This was wild and filled with adrenaline, like jumping out of a plane without a parachute. It was scary and exhilarating all at the same time. And I didn't want it to end.

But it did. One moment, we were in our own little world, our bodies colliding, and the next, the sounds of battle and the pain pulsing across my skin returned. I suddenly remembered where I was and what I was doing there.

A woman's high-pitched scream tore through the dungeon. My fingers tightened around Venn's arms. Both our heads snapped in the direction of the scream. It echoed in my ears over and over as sheer agony tore through my body.

Fiona was back in human form, and Maliya held her by the hair. Her dagger pressed into the skin on Fiona's neck.

"Stop!" Maliya shouted.

The entire room quieted. Everything was so still that all I could hear was the sound of Fiona's breathing. I glanced around me to see that two of Maliya's men remained. Cowen paused between Ryland and Teagan in the hall, his fangs bared. The other—the new vamp—was on top of Ryland, his massive biceps curled around Ryland's thick neck. Slowly, he loosened his hold on him and climbed off the bear. Ryland shifted back to human form but stood completely still. He stared at his sister with apology in his eyes.

"If you touch any more of my men, the girl dies," Maliya threatened.

A beat passed. If we moved, Fiona was dead.

If we don't do anything, we're all dead, I told myself.

"Cowen, Evan," Maliya instructed, "bring the other two in."

The new vamp, Evan, pushed Ryland down the hall. Cowen smirked as he grabbed ahold of Teagan's arm and shoved her through the door.

"Don't touch her!" Ryland roared.

"Shut up, or I'll hurt the girl," Maliya warned.

Ryland quieted and followed Evan into the room. His lips tightened, but there was a fire in his eyes that told me there was still a lot of fight left in him.

"Call Dreyfus," Maliya told Evan. "He needs to get his ass down here with all his men, and then he's fired."

Evan nodded and pulled a phone from his pocket.

"The rest of you…" Maliya snarled. She cocked her head toward the open cell I'd spent the night in. "Get inside."

Venn shot me a glance I couldn't read. We were out of time, and we all knew it. Our only options were to enter the cell or watch Fiona bleed out in front of us. I didn't care what they did to me after they locked me back up; I wouldn't be the reason she died.

Venn stepped forward before any of us had a chance to move. "Maliya…"

"Venn," Maliya said with a click of her tongue. "I was really hoping I didn't have to kill you."

Venn inched forward another step, testing her. Maliya's lips curled back over her teeth to reveal her fangs. Her dagger left Fiona's neck, and she pointed it at Venn.

"Take one more step," she dared him.

I suddenly realized what that look he'd shot me meant. He was buying us one more moment. It was now or never.

I didn't give it a second thought. I jumped forward and shifted mid-air. Before Maliya had a chance to react, my sharp beak clamped around her outstretched hand. She let out a scream, and the dagger fell to the ground with a *clink*.

The room exploded again. Venn shifted, and his powerful jaws sank into Maliya's ankle. My talons dug into her other hand. I squeezed harder and harder until she dropped Fiona's hair. And still I ripped at the flesh on her hand.

I didn't pay attention to what everyone else was doing. I could only guess Ryland and Teagan were dealing with the other two vamps. All that mattered to me in that moment was causing Maliya pain.

My talons clawed at Maliya's skin as she shrieked. I found pleasure in the feeling of my claws tearing through her flesh. I ripped at her hands, her face, and her chest—anything I could get. My talons caught on one of her necklaces. I tugged harder until the tension in the chain tore away. The necklace snapped off her neck and flew through the air away from us.

The sound of Venn's wolf whimper reached my ears.

No.

I turned to see what was going on, but all I saw was a fist flying at my face. Pain shot out across my entire head as I flew backward across the room, unable to control my trajectory. I slammed against the stone between two cells. I gasped for air that didn't come. I shifted back to human form, hoping that might help me catch my breath. When my head cleared, I looked up to see that Teagan was on Ryland's back. They were still taking on Evan with Fiona's help. Venn struggled to his feet. It looked like someone had targeted his ribs again to knock him down.

Cowen was at Maliya's side, supporting her as they raced past cells toward the open one on the end. Dave's keys dangled from Cowen's hand.

Beside me, Maliya's dagger caught my eye. I snatched it up from the ground with my good hand. Fury ignited throughout my body. My teeth gritted, and my eyebrows tightened. A scream ripped out of my lungs as I drew my arm back and hurled the dagger at Maliya's back.

It flipped over and over in the air. Maliya and Cowen reached the open cell, and Cowen swung the door shut. The dagger connected with the bars with a loud *clank* that echoed throughout the dungeon.

I scurried forward, my sights on the dagger. Before I could reach it, a pair of arms wrapped around my middle. I struggled against them, but it wasn't much use when I could hardly use my left arm.

"We have to go," Venn's voice came in my ear.

I instantly stopped struggling.

"They're coming," Venn cried. "We have to leave. Now."

He tugged at me again. I told my legs to move, but I couldn't tear my gaze away from Cowen. He stood in the middle of the cell with a wide, taunting smile on his face. He knew he'd won this battle. I wasn't getting past those bars before the rest of the vamps showed up and killed us.

"Come on!" Teagan's urgent voice filled the dungeon.

I tore my gaze from Cowen's, and my feet finally complied to my demands. I hurried to my feet beside Venn, and we raced behind Ryland, Teagan, and Fiona. My gaze flickered across the floor as we ran. A fresh pile of ash told me they'd killed Evan. And then my eyes caught a glimpse of a small object reflecting the candlelight.

The locket.

"Wait!" I cried, pulling against Venn.

He was still headed toward the door but didn't let go of my hand. I swore he almost pulled my shoulder out of the socket. He paused just long enough for me to scoop up the locket. I glanced back to the cell at the other end of the room just in time to see confusion cross Maliya's injured face. Her hands shot to her chest, and her face contorted in fury when she realized she no longer had the locket. Cowen realized the same thing a split second later and immediately began fumbling with the keys.

Looks like you didn't win this battle after all.

Venn and I sprinted down the hall, and Cowen and Maliya disappeared from view. We followed Ryland in his bear form up a flight of steps and then down another long hall. It was like a freaking maze in this mansion.

Finally, we broke out of the dark hallways leading to the

dungeon. My heart nearly stopped in my chest. When we reached one of the main halls, a swarm of vampires was headed our way, blocking our escape from the mansion.

Ryland didn't even hesitate. He bowed his head and barreled his way through the crowd. We sprinted closely behind him. Hands flung out toward me, but I dodged out of their way. Vampires screamed as we entered the main foyer. A marble floor stretched out in front of us, and the ceiling reached up three levels. The only piece of furniture was a small table at the center with a potted plant on top of it. The front doors looked miles away.

Suddenly, my legs seized, and I fell face-first into the ground as a vampire tackled me. As soon as I hit the floor, I regained control of my legs. I swung my foot out, and it connected with the vampire's nose.

Just as I managed to free myself from him, another set of hands grabbed me, a woman this time. She bared her fangs at me. I held the locket tight in my right fist and swung it up at her jaw. She stumbled back just enough that I managed to wiggle free. I rushed to my feet.

In front of me, Venn struggled against another vampire's hold. I sprinted forward and sank my teeth into the vampire's hand, clamping down as hard as I could. I didn't have sharp fangs, but it got the job done. The vampire leapt backward, freeing Venn. Pretty good for a girl whose left arm was out of commission.

Ahead of us, another vampire lunged forward and caught Fiona by the tail. She let out a yelp as the vampire dragged her backward across the floor. As we raced by the table at the center of the room, Venn grabbed the plant. He held it high over his head, then dropped it straight on the vamp's head.

Fiona scurried from his grasp. I scooped up Fiona's small body. We sprinted the remaining distance to the front doors and broke out into cool air behind Ryland and Teagan.

There was just a sliver of sunlight on the horizon, casting a dull glow over the landscape. I had no way of telling if it was dawn or twilight, because I didn't know how long I'd been writhing in pain on the floor of that cell.

My legs burned as we continued sprinting down the long driveway. I glanced behind me to see vampires flooding out of the front doors. Some quickly sank back into the safety of the house, while others sprinted into the sun rays, risking severe burns to pursue us. They advanced quickly.

Teagan aimed a knife at the closest one. It flipped through the air and sank into his chest. His body disintegrated into a pile of ash when he was only three feet from me.

"Good shot!" I called.

Teagan smiled in satisfaction then hurled another knife at an oncoming vamp. He too crumbled into a pile of ash behind us. Teagan reached for her hip, but despite the many sheaths that hung off her belt, her hands found nothing.

"I'm out!" she cried to Ryland just as we reached the perimeter wall. In one swift motion, she brought her knees up, pressed her heels into Ryland's back, and leapt off from him, scurrying over the wall.

Ryland turned and sprinted in the opposite direction, heading straight for the vampires behind us. His teeth bared, and his frightening roar sounded across the vast lawn. Venn jumped and caught the top of the wall and pulled himself up. He paused at the top and reached out his hand. I tossed Fiona up to him. Biting on to the locket chain, I shifted and flew over the wall. I stole one glance behind me to see Ryland swinging his massive head into three vampires at once, knocking them all off their feet.

Once he saw we were all over the wall, he turned and raced toward it. He reached up with his bear paws but pulled himself over in human form, landing with a *thud* in the grass on the other side.

"Come on!" Venn shouted.

Everyone sprinted behind Venn through the trees while I flew above them, dodging tree branches as I went. The adrenaline helped me push past the pain in my left wing. I didn't look behind me this time to see if we had any followers. A break in the trees loomed ahead, where I saw Venn's car parked along the edge of the road.

We all scurried inside. Venn, Fiona, and I were in the back, and Ryland was in the passenger seat. Teagan twisted the key in the ignition. Tires squealed as we made our escape.

I shifted back into human form and glanced behind us. Two vampires had made it through the scorching sun and were pursuing us, but they couldn't keep up with Teagan's increasing speed.

Finally, I had a chance to catch my breath, though my heart hammered. It only served to push the pain of the venom faster through my body.

"Everyone okay?" Ryland asked through heavy breaths.

"We're alive," Venn said, like that was all that mattered. He clutched on to his side.

I wanted nothing more than to help. I reached for him, but he just shook his head.

"Rae's bleeding," Fiona said with worry. I barely remembered the blood but saw that it was still oozing out of the wounds on my arm.

Ryland flung open the glove compartment and tossed us a stack of napkins. Fiona took half the stack and pressed it to my arm to slow the bleeding.

"What now?" Teagan asked. "What's our next move?"

I held out the locket in my hand. "Can we use this to decide what to do next?"

"You got it!" Fiona squeaked.

"Please tell me it's the locket you were looking for," I begged. I didn't want all that to be for nothing. I offered her the locket while I took over wound duty.

Fiona gently took it. "Yes, this is it."

"Sondra taught you how to use it, didn't she?" Teagan asked.

Fiona nodded in excitement.

"Then use it," Ryland instructed. "Figure out if we can go home."

Fiona went to put the locket around her neck but quickly realized the clasp was broken. Instead, she held the locket tight in her hand and closed her eyes.

"It works for anyone?" I asked Venn while Fiona concentrated. "Not just witches?"

Venn nodded, though the movement appeared strained. "That's why it's valuable to vampires, since they can't conduct magic of their own."

"They're coming after us," Fiona stated. "But it'll take them a while to find us. They have to go through some contacts to track us down. We have until dawn."

"Okay, here's what we'll do," Ryland said with a tone of authority. "We'll head home and pack up what we can. We'll leave before daylight and head straight for Matias's. We'll figure out our next move once we have Sondra. Sound good?"

Everyone nodded in unison.

"Okay, let's—" Ryland didn't get a chance to finish his sentence.

Beside me, Venn's face went pale, and his eyes rolled back in his head.

He was out cold.

20

"How are you feeling?" My voice was hoarse. An hour had passed since Venn had blacked out. I was just glad he was alive and healing.

He pushed himself up to a sitting position on his bed and glanced around. Venn's room was clean, but otherwise totally not what I expected. The navy-blue color scheme made sense, but then there was a bookcase along one wall filled with fiction books. An acoustic guitar was situated on a stand in the corner. I wouldn't have pegged him for a reader or a musician. Learning he was both… well, it was kind of hot.

I'd walked around the room while he was sleeping, after I'd performed the healing spell on his ribs. We weren't entirely sure why he passed out, but my guess was because it'd gotten hard to breathe.

While I explored his room, I found a picture of him in a frame on the dresser. He looked around twelve. He stood with his arm around another boy who looked several years younger than him but had the same dark skin tone and full lips.

Above the dresser, three hand drawings were taped to the wall. They looked a lot like the ones in the hall, so I guessed Sondra had drawn them. The pictures showed different poses of a couple hugging. The guy was tall, with dark skin, and the girl pale with long dark hair. I couldn't see their faces in any of the pictures, but I thought for sure the guy was Venn.

I didn't want to ask who the girl was. She could've been an old girlfriend or something.

It was interesting, to say the least, to be in Venn's bedroom. It was like I knew him better now.

Eventually, Venn's eyes fell on me seated in the big comfy chair by his closet. A hint of a smile touched his lips. "I'm feeling better, actually. I guess I have you to thank for that."

My cheeks flushed, and I nodded. What the heck? I wasn't the blushing kind of girl.

I stood on shaky feet, ignoring the fire raging through my sore muscles. I crossed the room to the duffel bag in front of his dresser. "I was hoping you'd wake up soon so you could tell me what to pack for you."

Venn glanced to the empty duffel bag. "You don't have to do that."

"I do," I insisted. "You're still healing."

Venn pulled the covers aside, revealing his toned torso. Bruises splayed across his skin, but with the healing spell, they were already starting to look better. It would take a couple of days until he was back to normal, though. He stood, as if to prove a point.

I rushed over to him and pushed on his shoulders. "Venn, you—"

He grabbed my wrists gently. His touch was like an electric shock, and not just because my arm was still prickling with searing pain from the vampire venom.

"I'm fine, Rae," he whispered.

He stared down at me, his eyes flickering to my lips. Oh, how I would love to kiss him again, but I couldn't. I shouldn't have kissed him in the first place. It was a huge mistake, because now I felt... I felt things I shouldn't be feeling. I couldn't get attached. I mean, Venn didn't even know my real name.

"Rachel," I said breathlessly. The name slipped out before I could stop myself. I cleared my throat and repeated my name. At least if he knew it, we might be able to find each other again... someday. "Rachel Collins," I said. "That's my name."

A smile crept across his face, widening slowly. "I like it. It's a pretty name."

Heart. Officially. Melted. And not because he gave me a compliment. That smile was to die for.

Our eyes locked, and my gaze traveled down to his lips. Now that he knew my name, it couldn't hurt to—

No, I scolded myself. I barely knew him. For starters, there was clear history between Venn and Maliya. And it'd be insanely rude to ask about.

"What's the story with you and Maliya?"

Holy crap! Where had that come from? My mouth wasn't supposed to work without my consent!

Venn tensed for a moment, then dropped my hands. He stepped around me to his duffel bag and opened the top dresser drawer. He riffled through it and pulled out clothes to shove into his bag, all without looking me in the eye.

"I thought you would've figured it out by now," he said tensely.

I bit my lower lip and sank onto the bed. "I have a good guess. If it's what I think it is, I'm really sorry, Venn."

He tossed a pile of clothes into his bag. "Don't be. It's not your fault."

I wasn't going to push it. It wasn't fair of me to dig into his past like this. "I'm sorry. I didn't mean to bring it up."

He paused and then shrugged. "It's not a secret. It's pretty obvious. I was her blood slave."

Holy crap! I'd assumed he was a blood slave in her house, but the way he said it… *her* blood slave. He'd been her personal pet. The thought made me want to vomit. I forced down the lump in my throat.

"I know what you're thinking," he said solemnly.

"What am I thinking?" I asked curiously.

Venn took a deep breath. "You must think the worst of me. You must be wondering why I stayed."

"Of course I don't think any less of you," I assured him. "You were forced to stay."

"Yeah, but I wanted to," he admitted without meeting my eyes.

He *wanted* to?

Venn ran his fingers through his hair and returned to packing. "Most people are very judgmental. They don't get what it's like to be fed on."

"It's like a drug, isn't it? For both of you." I remembered what it felt like the moment Dracula sank his teeth into my neck. It was blissful. Addicting.

Venn nodded, slowly folding clothes into his bag. "It's… a hard habit to break."

"How'd you end up with her?"

I shouldn't have been asking these personal things. My mouth apparently had no filter.

Venn hesitated.

"Never mind," I said. "You don't have to tell me."

"I know." He finally turned to me, a look of sadness in his eyes. "But the crazy thing is that I want to tell you. I want you to know. It's just… hard to talk about."

"Then don't worry about it," I told him. "Really, Venn. I don't want—"

"My parents fell into a bad deal with a group of shifters when I was fourteen," he interrupted. "They died."

My heart sank. Of course. Because everyone here had lost their parents. It didn't seem right.

"My brother and I went to live with my grandfather," Venn continued. "It was… not the best situation. My grandfather was just as emotionally abusive to us as he was to my dad. But I had to stay… for my brother."

Venn zipped his bag and sighed. He crossed the room and sat on his bed beside me. "We lived there for about a year before my brother was attacked by a vampire and changed."

My hand shot over my mouth. I couldn't believe all these terrible things had happened to him. Why was he telling me all this?

"I left. Maliya found me not long after that. Believe it or not, she treated me well… at first. It was only after she had my trust that she started to show her true side. But it was still a warm bed to sleep in."

Tears welled in my eyes. I thought my past was horrible, but it was nothing compared to the story he just told me. I couldn't imagine.

"Luckily, Sondra came along as things started to get worse," Venn said.

"She saved you?" I asked in a small voice.

Venn nodded. "She was working a deal with Maliya, but Sondra refused monetary payment. She ended up trading me for payment instead."

I didn't know it was possible for my heart to break any further. It wasn't fair that Venn had gone through all that. He didn't deserve it. He deserved happiness and love.

I didn't know what I was doing when I reached out to touch him. My hands ran over his exposed shoulders. A tingle spread through my body upon contact. He gazed down at my arms, his eyes slowly drifting past the bandages until they landed on my hands. A hint of a smile touched his lips, like he welcomed my touch. I gently wrapped my arms around him, and he rested his head on mine. His body heat was strangely comforting. I didn't know how I could sit there with him feeling so comfortable, like this was where I was meant to be.

Now's not the time to get attached, I reminded myself. But I didn't pull away. I let myself enjoy the moment. I forgot how good it felt to hold someone, to be held.

Venn took a long breath. "Anyway, I've been with the family ever since. What about you? How'd you get here?"

I was shocked by the question, but for some reason, it felt perfectly natural opening up to Venn—like we'd had conversations like this a million times before.

"I grew up in a really close family," I said, surprised to hear the words tumbling out of my mouth with such ease. "It was just me, my sister, and my mom and dad. My life was basically perfect before the vampires came."

Memories of that night flickered through my mind. The screams. The blood. The mark of the Soulless.

I swallowed hard. "When I was sixteen, a group of vampires raided my house in the middle of the night. I heard my parents' screams downstairs. I remember shaking in fear. I'd never felt so scared in my life. That was the first time I shifted."

I took a deep breath as images flickered across the back of

my closed lids. I remembered a vampire's voice from Jenna's room. *'No, she's mine,'* he said. The sound of her voice shrieking at me to run… A vampire barged into my room, but I was in raven form, crouched into the small space between my bookcase and the ceiling. The vampire flipped my mattress and pulled my closet door off its track. I remembered how he reached up to the bookshelf I was on. His hand getting so close to me, the mark of the Soulless coming closer and closer… I remembered how I thought he'd found me. He just knocked all the books off the top shelf instead. He never saw me.

But I didn't tell Venn any of that. I didn't want him to know I was after the Soulless. He'd want to protect me from them.

"I tried to follow them when they took Jenna, but they piled in this van and disappeared." A sob broke out in my chest, but I held the tears back. I shouldn't be crying. I was stronger than that.

"It's okay," Venn told me, readjusting so that he held me close to his chest.

I wanted to tell him it wasn't, but in his arms, I could almost believe it was okay. It felt as if a huge weight had lifted off my shoulders when I shared my story. It was different than when I'd told Fiona. Fiona got the vague, watered-down version, but with Venn, all the memories came rushing back as if I was reliving them.

I sniffled and wiped the tears from my eyes. "The police investigated my family's murder, but the vampires responsible were never caught. I had no other family, so I was put into foster care. I was only there a few months before I filed for emancipation and moved to the city. My landlord gave me a deal on my apartment."

Though, my landlord was a pig who raised my rent as soon as I turned eighteen. I was sure it was because I wouldn't indulge in his advances. I didn't mention that to Venn.

I shrugged. "One thing led to another, I started killing vampires on my off-hours, and here I am."

Venn pulled me even tighter and placed a warm kiss on my forehead.

Damn it. He was going to make it hard to leave. I wanted to be close to him. I wanted to get to know him better. I wanted to stay with this family because for the first time in years, I finally felt like I belonged.

And that scared the hell out of me.

"I'm so sorry," Venn whispered, the sound of his voice melodic, entrancing.

Before I knew what I was doing, my body leaned into him as if magnetized. My lips brushed against his. The kiss was like magic, melting away the pain in my veins and making me feel as if I was floating. Venn kissed me back, and desire ignited deep in my belly. I parted my lips, inviting him to deepen the kiss. His tongue grazed against my lower lip. For a moment, all was perfect in the world.

And then reality came crashing down on me.

"No!" I pushed him away and sprang to my feet.

He stared back at me with utter shock, as if to ask what he'd done wrong.

"I—I'm sorry." My voice shook. "I just can't do this."

"Rae," Venn whispered, reaching out for me.

I took another step back. "I'm sorry, Venn. I've already lost too many people I love."

Venn bit his lower lip. "You're saying you don't want to lose me, either?"

I wasn't sure what I was saying, but that was a pretty darn good way of putting it into words.

I nodded. "I can't go with you, Venn."

He didn't say anything for a long time. My chest started to hurt as I stared down at his wounded expression. *I'm sorry* didn't even begin to cover it.

He finally lifted his head. "What will you do without us?"

I considered his question for a moment. I was leaving the city. I knew that much. But I was leaving alone.

I sat back down beside him. "I'm going after my sister."

I didn't know how I was getting to Seattle, but assuming Cowen made his flight Maliya mentioned, that's where I'd find him. And he was my only lead on Jenna. One way or another, I'd get to him.

After a beat, Venn spoke softly. "I don't want you to go alone."

"But I have to," I countered. "You have Sondra, and I have my sister. I can take care of myself."

"I know. You told me that the night we met."

It already felt like a million years ago.

"Stay with us, Rae," Venn begged.

I shook my head. "I don't think I can."

"You can't go alone," he whispered. "Is there nothing I can say that'll make you come with us?"

He was already saying all the things that could make me stay, but I fought against them.

I shook my head. "I can handle myself, Venn. Don't worry about me."

"I'm going to worry," he promised.

Damn it. Why was this so hard?

"I have to go," I insisted. "Alone. I can't stay here, and you can't come with me."

I knew I was being unfair. His family just risked their necks for me, and I repaid them by hitting the road. But my only choices were to walk away from them or walk away from Jenna. Guilt twisted in my gut, wrenching at my insides so fiercely that it almost overshadowed the venom.

"Yes, I can," he insisted. "I can—"

"Venn," I cut him off. "This isn't up for discussion. I've been on my own for years. I'll be fine."

Venn sighed. "I just want to be with you, Rae… I want to keep you safe."

The guy was tempting as hell.

"Please don't treat me like I'm incapable of making my own decisions," I said, tears welling in my eyes.

Sorrow crossed Venn's eyes. He still didn't want me to go, but he knew he couldn't stop me. He had no choice but to give in.

"I hope you find what you're looking for," he whispered. "If you ever feel like your journey is over, you can always come find us."

I cracked a smile. "Thank you."

Venn stood and crossed over to his dresser. He grabbed a pen that lay there and returned to my side. He scribbled a number on the palm of my hand. "There's my phone number. And if you can't reach me there, take this."

He held an object so small in his hands that I couldn't see it. I held out my palm to accept his offer. He placed a piece of blue plastic the size of a quarter in my hand. A guitar pick.

"You don't get to keep it," Venn said.

Of course not. How could I find him if I claimed it as mine?

He reached out and curled my fingers around it. "I want it back. When you find me."

I pressed my lips together to keep the tears from falling. I nodded. Damn him. Why was he making it so hard to leave?

A light knock came at the door. I quickly dashed the tears away.

"Come in," Venn called.

Fiona stuck her head inside the room. "Oh, good. You're up. I was just wondering if you needed anything."

Venn shook his head. "I have a few more things to pack, and then I'm going to take Rae home."

Fiona's face fell. "You're leaving?"

I nodded because I couldn't bear to speak. I bet I could've been really good friends with Fiona.

"But we just…" Fiona stared at me like a deer in the headlights. After a beat, she crossed the room and pulled me into a hug. "We're going to miss you, Rae."

"Don't be silly." My voice cracked. "You just met me."

She drew away and wiped at her eyes. "Maybe in this life, but I feel like I've known you forever. We all do."

It was strange how I felt the same way about them.

Maybe I should stay, I thought.

I pictured myself with the family, leaving the city and leading that quiet life they talked about. In my mind, I rocked on a porch swing. Fiona sat curled up next to me in her fox form, and Sondra sat in a chair nearby sketching the landscape. The sun was high in the sky, spreading happiness across our property. The wind gently rustled through my hair. The wrap-around porch we sat on overlooked a wide-open lawn that stretched out to a line of trees that blocked our view of the quiet road. In the distance, Ryland and Teagan tended to our garden, and their future son pedaled his tricycle down the driveway. The strum of Venn's guitar and the melodic sound of his voice filled the air. He smiled at me from where he sat playing on the steps. Everything was perfect... except Jenna wasn't there.

I returned to the present. It was clear to me now why I was doing this. If Jenna was still out there, I'd never find her if I went with the family. And I'd never be happy with them without closure.

"Are you ready to go?" Venn asked.

As much as it broke my heart, it was time to leave.

21

It was incredible how you could feel so strongly for someone you just met. I sat on my bed alone in my apartment, rolling Venn's guitar pick around in my fingers. I couldn't stop thinking about him, about leaving him.

The pain in my muscles had eased to a dull ache. There must've not been as much venom on Maliya's blade as I thought. My bag sat beside me, packed and ready to go. I didn't have many belongings, so it only took me five minutes or so to pack everything up.

All I needed to do was leave my key on the table and slip the note I'd written under my landlord's door explaining I was leaving and he could lease the room to someone else. Luckily, he was lazy with his record keeping, so he wouldn't have much luck tracking me down for unpaid rent on the contract. I'd take what cash I had and head to the bus station, where I'd hop on a bus to Chicago and take the first flight to Seattle. There, I'd find Cowen and get answers.

And yet, I couldn't bring myself to actually rise to my feet and leave. It wasn't like I was attached to this place. I mean, I just used it as somewhere to crash and keep my stuff. It barely fulfilled its purpose. At least I was able to get a shower one last time. I wasn't sure when I'd see a bed or a shower again. It could be weeks.

But it still felt like I was leaving something behind. I racked my brain, trying to think if I'd hidden anything in the cupboards or behind a baseboard, but I figured if something was valuable enough to hide, I would remember it. I wouldn't miss this creaky old bed, the pipes that made noises every time I turned on the faucet, or the water stain on the ceiling. I wouldn't miss my job, though Devin deserved a phone call to know I quit. About the only thing I'd miss was patrolling. It was the only time I ever felt something. Before I met Venn, of course.

That was what was holding me back.

I wasn't ready to take a break from slaying vampires… from being the Ravenite.

One more night, I told myself.

The last night I went patrolling, I ran into Cowen, and he got away. I wouldn't let that be my final fight in Nocton. This city may've sucked as bad as Hell's armpit, but for the last two years, it'd been my home. The people here deserved one last fight from the Ravenite.

I shot up from my bed. Fiona said I had until morning. I wouldn't let tonight be a night I'd forget. I was going to find the biggest, baddest vamp I could, and I was going to kick his ass. It would be my greatest fight yet.

***

I sat perched on the roof of Red Whiskey, knowing that if I

was going to find a vampire worth killing, this was as good of place as any to hunt one down.

So far, the night was a total bust.

I was disappointed, and frankly a little bored, but my determination hadn't waned. A vampire *would* die by my hand tonight. I'd wait all night if I had to.

The sidewalk in front of the bar was quiet, apart from the heavy bass shaking the building and spilling out onto the street every time someone opened the door. It was a slow night, nothing compared to last Friday when the street was buzzing with nightlife.

A group of people—humans, it looked like from this distance—walked along on the other side of the street. Other than that, there wasn't much to see. If there was anything worth watching, it was all going on inside the bar.

Which was why I decided I should check it out. I never admitted to being the sharpest tool in the box, but this girl really needed to see some vampire action or she was going to lose it.

I swooped down into the alley and shifted. I peeked around the corner of the building, but there was no one close enough to see me slip out of the shadows.

The music pulsed through me like a bass drum when I stepped inside Red Whiskey. It was like the building had completely transformed since I was in here last. There were fewer tables than before—all thanks to Ryland, I'm sure—so most people stood and danced. Women wore short skirts and held their drinks in the air. Most of their glasses were filled with a thick red liquid, and they sure as hell weren't Bloody Marys.

I was about to sit at the bar, but then I spotted Kieren and immediately turned in the other direction. I'd probably get thrown out if he saw me. I threw myself into the crowd so I wouldn't be seen. Bodies pressed in on me. I swayed my hips to the music to blend in.

"Hey," a girl beside me called over the music. She had long blonde hair, pale skin, and silver eyes. She held a red drink in her hand and moved her hips expertly to the beat of the music. "You looking for someone?"

I hadn't realized I'd been that obvious scanning the crowd.

"My friends," I lied.

"You can dance with us until they come back," she offered. The hot vampire lady grabbed my wrist with her cold fingers and pulled me toward her group of friends.

What was I doing? They probably wanted to eat me alive.

The girl swayed her hips beside me, bumping into me every so often.

"Come on," she encouraged. "You're not scared of me, are you?"

Hell no! I just wasn't used to dancing like this. Heck, I hardly ever danced at all. This girl knew what she was doing with her hips, and I'd been wondering how to use mine since puberty hit.

Vampire Girl grabbed my hand and held it up above my head. I twirled for her, but my eyes remained on the crowd. So far, no one caught my eye.

She laughed when I completed my twirl and faced her. "You from around here?"

"What?" I shouted over the music.

My eyes locked on a group of three guys who'd all stopped dancing. They glanced down at a phone then back up, scanning the crowd like they were nervous.

"I said, are you from around here?" she repeated.

I barely processed what she'd said. "Huh? Oh, I'm sorry. I think I see my friends. It was good dancing with you."

She winked at me. "Feel free to come back if your friends aren't any fun. I'll show you a good time."

It wasn't until I pushed through the crowd and was halfway across the bar that I realized she'd been hitting on me. Weird.

The guys I had my eye on hurried off the dancefloor and down the hall that led to the bathrooms, where there was some relief from the music.

I followed behind them and dropped my head. My hair fell in front of my face as I pushed myself into the girl's bathroom. It was empty, so I didn't feel weird about opening the door a crack and peeking through it to spy on the three guys. Two had silver eyes, but the other guy's were dark brown. My guess was he was either a shifter gone bad or a blood slave. With his strong build and smug expression, he certainly seemed to fit into the vampire crowd. Maybe these three would be worth taking out tonight.

"What'd she say?" the short vampire asked.

"Maliya found them," the taller vampire said.

All the blood drained from my face. *Please don't let him mean what I think he means.* I thought the family had until tomorrow. I listened as closely as I could, ignoring the music.

"She wants everyone but Cowen to report to the location now," the tall vampire said.

"What's Cowen doing?" the guy with brown eyes asked.

"He's headed to round up some old friends on Valander," Tall Vamp replied.

I swear my heart stopped. That was where we'd gone before, where Kieren had led us and Teagan got bit. I could easily intercept him on his way and finally get the information I needed from him. But—

"I'll let the others know," Short Vamp said. "What's the address we're supposed to meet at?"

I held my breath, praying he wouldn't say the address running through my mind. Every muscle in my body froze when the words I'd been dreading left his lips. *112 Amore Drive.*

Venn.

They'd found the family, but it was too soon. Fiona said they had until morning. Then I remembered what she told me about the future. It wasn't written in stone, which meant something had changed.

"Anything else?" Short Vamp asked.

"Yeah," Tall Vamp said. "Leave no survivors."

I dropped the door handle and stumbled back several paces, knocking over the garbage can. My gut twisted, and I thought I might puke. I almost tripped over my own feet as I crossed the room and caught myself on the counter. I braced myself over the sink, and my arms shook. This couldn't be happening. I had to warn them.

I reached for my pocket before I realized I didn't have my phone on me. Of course not. It wouldn't shift with me. I never brought it on patrol.

Voices passed the door, snapping me back to attention. They were headed to round up Maliya's cronies. I needed to get out of here. I rushed across the room to the door, but before I could reach the handle, the door swung open. Vampire Girl from earlier nearly ran into me.

"Hey," she said with a smile. "You again. You ready to bring your friends over and dance?"

"I—I have to go." I pushed past her and into the hall. I

raced to the end and blasted out the exit. I didn't check to see if anyone was watching as I shifted and flapped my wings, launching into the air.

It took me several seconds to realize which direction I was headed. I was flying in the direction of Valander, toward where Cowen was supposed to be. It was a closer flight, and I could be there in a matter of minutes. I couldn't stop thinking about Jenna, how if I got what I wanted from Cowen, I'd finally be able to find out what happened to my sister.

But then images of Venn invaded my mind. His soft, familiar eyes, his full lips and gorgeous smile, the warmth of his embrace…

It didn't make sense for me to want to save someone I'd just met over my own *sister*, but at the same time, it seemed like the only rational course of action. Jenna had been gone for two years. I wasn't even sure if she was still alive. If I didn't act *now*, I was certain that Venn and his family wouldn't make it.

I hesitated a moment longer.

Screw it. I have to warn Venn.

I just hoped I wasn't too late.

22

I was in such a hurry that I couldn't slow my momentum when I came in for the landing. My entire body slammed against the glass window at the front of the house. I dropped to the porch, heaving in deep breaths. I shifted back into human form where I lay. Every muscle in my body ached.

"Oh, my God! What are you doing out here, Rae?" Fiona's voice reached my ears as she rushed outside.

"I—I needed to—to warn you," I managed to spit out between heavy breaths.

Fiona helped pull me to my feet. "Warn us? Rae, what's going on?"

I finally steadied myself on two feet and caught my breath. "They're coming here. Now."

"But the locket showed me—"

"Something changed."

Fiona's entire body froze, and her eyes went wide. She whirled around and raced back into the house. I followed quickly behind her.

"It's time to go!" she shouted up the stairs.

Fiona hurried down the hall and flung open the cupboard beneath the stairs. My jaw dropped when I saw the pile of weapons hanging from the walls. Guns, daggers, axes… There was even a sword and a crossbow with a full quiver attached. It looked high-tech, like the kind that auto-cocked itself.

Fiona caught the look on my face while she grabbed for the weapons. "We don't get much chance to use them since we prefer fighting in our shifted form. And Teagan would rather use her knives."

Fiona shoved the handle of a dagger into my hands. It was completely silver, with intricate designs carved into the blade. She took a gun for herself, an old-style revolver that only held six bullets. She quickly checked the chamber to confirm it was full, then cocked the firing pin before grabbing the crossbow.

I glanced down at the dagger in my hand, my heart pounding. "You don't understand. You can't fight them. They're coming with all they've got. They're going to kill you. You have to leave now!"

Footsteps pounded down the stairs. Venn stopped at the bottom, and his eyes locked on me. A smile touched the corner of his lips, like he was glad to see me. Which totally would've melted my heart if he wasn't about to be ambushed.

Fiona glanced up at him. "You have twenty seconds to get the rest of the bags in the car. Rae says the vamps are on their way."

"What?" Venn gawked. "How do you—?"

"No time to explain," I said. "You all have to leave immediately."

"You wanna go bad-ass wolf shifter, or do you want to play slayer?" Fiona asked Venn.

"What's going on?" Ryland demanded as he descended the

stairs with Teagan close behind him. "I thought we had another few hours."

Fiona tossed the crossbow up, and Teagan caught it.

"Something changed," I said in a rush. "You're out of time—"

As if on cue, the front door burst open, sending slivers of busted door frame flying across the front hall. Ryland and Venn shifted before I could blink. Fiona pulled the trigger on her gun, and a loud *pop* cracked through the air. Teagan brought the bow to her shoulder in an instant.

Ryland lunged forward, and the bodies of the closest vampires flew backward through the door. His huge bear form blocked any others from getting through. The sound of shattering glass and the pumped-up roar of invading vampires filled the living room.

"Run!" Teagan screamed.

I sprinted as fast as I could down the hall, never looking back as I hightailed it to the back door near the kitchen. My blood ran cold and I stopped in my tracks when a scream of terror erupted from Teagan's lungs. Fiona and I whirled around just in time to see a vampire with his arms wrapped around Teagan, his fangs headed for her throat. Three others were already racing down the hall toward me, while dozens more flooded in through the broken window in the living room.

I didn't hesitate a moment. I rushed forward and sank the dagger into the closest vampire's chest. I didn't wait around to watch him disintegrate into a pile of ash. My dagger was already speeding toward the chest of the next vampire.

Fiona got off five more shots. I saw several vamps turn to ash out of the corner of my eye, but I didn't count how many. Fiona dropped her gun once she was out of bullets. She grabbed a picture frame off the wall and swung it toward the closest vampire's head. The glass in the frame shattered. She swooped down and snatched up the sharpest fracture and stabbed it straight into the vampire's chest.

Ahead of us, Teagan had dropped her crossbow and was holding a knife in either hand. She swung her arm backward, slicing her knife through a nearby vampire's eye. He screamed and stumbled backward. Teagan whirled around and sank her other knife into his chest. I still couldn't believe this girl was only human.

Meanwhile, Ryland and Venn had pushed the vampires at the door outside. I couldn't see them, but their growls told me they were still alive. For how much longer, I didn't know. All I knew was that I couldn't let this family die. I had to help them make their escape.

Fiona reached back inside the cupboard under the stairs and grabbed the sword. She sliced it through the air, nicking a vamp's neck when he tried to grab her. I'd plunged a knife into two other vampires' chests by the time I made it to the front door.

Outside, dozens of vampires flooded the front lawn, and there were only more coming from down the street. When the vamps said Maliya wanted *everyone* to attack the house, they weren't kidding. She'd called in every favor she could.

There was no way we were making it out of here alive. It only made me want to fight harder. It didn't matter what Maliya did to me; she wasn't taking this family down, too.

Three vampires jumped Venn at the same time. His sharp teeth sank into one of the vampire's hands. The vamp screamed, and his face contorted in pain. I realized the moment I saw him that I recognized his large frame and dark hair. He was the Alpha Vamp who had bitten Teagan. The whole lot of them were back to get their revenge on us.

I sprinted across the porch and jumped the banister to reach Venn as fast as I could. One vampire had ahold of Venn, while the other swung a foot at his face to force his jaws off Alpha Vamp's hand. Venn let out a whimper.

The vampires never saw me coming. I jumped down off the porch and sank my dagger into the back of the nearest vampire, the one who held Venn down. The second vamp whirled toward me, just in time for my blade to enter his chest.

Venn rolled over in the grass, finally free of the vampires. Alpha Vamp completely forgot about him as his eyes, etched in fury, turned to me. Before I could get out of the way, he lunged. His strong fingers clamped around my throat, and my body crashed to the ground. A satisfied smirk spread across his face as I gasped for air. Pain filled my chest, and my vision clouded. I thought for sure this was the end.

Then a howl cut through the night, and a shadow flashed in front of my eyes. Alpha Vamp's weight lifted off of me, and air filled my lungs again.

I sat up, sputtering. "Venn!"

I tossed my dagger into the grass two feet away from him. It stuck into the earth right where I'd been aiming. Venn shifted back into human form and grabbed it. Alpha Vamp didn't have time to react before Venn shoved the blade into his chest. Alpha Vamp crumbled into a pile of ash.

Venn rushed over to me as I jumped to my feet. Most of the vampires had made it into the house now. I glanced to Ryland on the front lawn. Nausea slammed into my gut so hard that if Venn hadn't been there to steady me, I would've fallen right back down. Time seemed to slow as the scene played out in front of me.

Four vampires wrestled Ryland in his bear form. I spotted Cowen among them. He threw himself onto Ryland's back but made the mistake of getting within reach of Ryland's powerful jaws. Ryland's sharp teeth clamped around Cowen's leg, and he whipped his body around. Cowen landed with an audible *thud* in the grass. His scream echoed through the air, but it was silenced by the weight of Ryland's strong paws pressing down on his chest.

Ryland's teeth ripped at the flesh on Cowen's neck. Pieces of skin went flying, exposing the raw flesh and bones beneath it. It was horrifying to watch. Ryland took one final swipe at him, severing his head from his shoulders. Cowen crumbled into a pile of dust on the front lawn.

My body shook, and I thought I might vomit. But it wasn't just horrifying to watch the gruesome death unfold before my eyes. With it, I watched the mark of the Soulless on Cowen's wrist vanish. I watched my one chance at finding out what happened to my sister disappear like dust in the wind. Any sliver of hope I had for Jenna perished in that moment.

An unsteadiness consumed me. I fell to my knees in the grass. Venn's voice swam in and out of focus. I was sure his hands were on me, but I couldn't feel him anymore.

It was over.

Somewhere beyond the dizziness, I heard the sickening crunch of breaking bones and Ryland's roar of pain. Four vampires leapt on top of him, twisting and pulling his limbs in different directions.

My stomach bottomed out. We were done for.

"Don't kill him!"

Maliya's voice sounded like it was coming from under water. She emerged from the house in her velvet, long-sleeved dress. She walked with grace but wore a tight expression on her face. The wounds I'd slashed across her face with my talons were barely visible. Damn vampire healing abilities. The image of her descending the porch steps swam in and out of focus.

"Don't kill him... yet," Maliya repeated. "I want them all out here. Now."

Four vampires followed out of the house, each of them holding on to one of my friends' arms. Teagan struggled against the two vampires dragging her outside, while Fiona remained still, tears streaming down her face. Their weapons were nowhere to be seen.

The feeling of strong hands snatching me up from the ground sent a shot of adrenaline through my chest. Venn shouted curses from beside me. Suddenly, the world came back into focus.

At least two sets of hands clung on to me and forced me forward. I stumbled into the porch light illuminating the lawn. I tried to struggle out of their grasp, but I'd lost my strength. Even shifting wouldn't save me now, and if it did, I'd never be able to save the rest of them.

"Ah, Venn," Maliya said with a smile when she turned to see her henchmen dragging us toward her. "Nice of you to join us."

The vampires forced me and Venn to our knees beside Ryland. He lay in the grass in his human form, his left arm twisted in an unnatural direction. His face was pale, and his eyes were closed.

Please don't be dead, I thought.

Maliya's henchmen positioned Teagan and Fiona on the opposite side of Ryland so that we all knelt in a line. I could see at least a dozen other vampires inside the house, moving by the windows as they raided the place.

They're going to kill us off one by one and make the rest of us watch, I thought. I wasn't sure I could stomach it.

One of the vamps ripped the dagger from Venn's grasp and threw it several yards away. Venn's lips curled, and his nostrils flared. He glared at Maliya with pure hostility.

Maliya paced in front of us. "You all know why we're here. You stole something from me."

"You stole it from us first," Teagan snapped.

Maliya glared at her, but the corners of her lips slowly turned up. "Yes, I suppose I did. And I want it back."

Teagan turned her face away when Maliya leaned down to run a manicured finger across her cheek. The touch was harmless, but I knew she was doing it to scare Teagan. Despite Teagan's tough exterior, it looked like it was working.

"Tell me, *human*," Maliya spat at her, "where can I find the locket?"

"I don't know." Teagan's voice shook.

Maliya's palm cracked across the side of Teagan's face. My stomach sank, but Teagan barely let it show it bothered her.

"She's telling the truth!" Fiona burst. "Ryland had the locket tonight, and you knocked him out."

"I didn't ask you, filthy fox!" Maliya roared.

Fiona flinched.

Maliya straightened. "I don't have all night to have my men search your entire house. So I'll give you three guesses on where you think the bear left the locket."

Teagan narrowed her eyes at Maliya. "Screw you."

This time, Maliya's hand missed Teagan entirely and exploded across Fiona's cheek. Fiona let out a cry. A red welt in the shape of Maliya's fingers grew on Fiona's skin. I winced. She was going to torture Fiona to make Teagan talk, and there was nothing I could do to help.

"One guess down, two to go," Maliya mocked.

"Stop it, Maliya," Venn demanded. I'd never heard him speak with such commanding authority before. "We'll give you the locket as soon as Ryland wakes. It's not worth any of our lives."

Laughter bubbled up from Maliya's chest. "Oh, honey," she sang in condescension. "You know how the rules go. I don't negotiate. We do this on *my* terms."

"We don't know where he put it," Venn growled.

Maliya smirked. "Then the girl better use her best educated guess."

Teagan tightened her lips, but she didn't speak.

"You're running out of time," Maliya mocked.

Teagan took a deep breath, as if fighting against her fury.

"Try the room at the top of the stairs, in the black bag next to the dresser."

Maliya gestured to one of her cronies. He raced inside to check it out.

"I can't promise you it's there," Teagan said.

"Then you better make your next guess count," Maliya snarled.

Venn leaned over, closing the few inches between us. His warm skin touched mine. Though he didn't say anything, I knew what he'd say if he could.

It's going to be okay, Rae.

Except it wasn't. We were drastically outnumbered. It would take a miracle.

"It's not here." The vampire who'd gone inside returned, holding on to an empty black duffel bag. All the contents had been emptied, and the pockets had been turned inside out.

Maliya's face remained expressionless, like she was an expert at hiding her true emotions. She paced slowly in front of us until she stopped in front of Venn. She gazed down at him past her nose. With a sudden burst of energy, her knee swung up and clipped his jaw.

I let out a shocked cry as Venn's body whipped backward. I tried to get to my feet, but the vampire behind me held my shoulders down and twisted my arms around my back. My knees sank into the earth. The two vampires guarding Venn slammed their fists into his face over and over again. A foot sank into his ribs, and he cried out. I knew his ribs hadn't healed yet, so the blow must've hurt like hell.

"Stop it!" I screamed.

"Please don't!" Fiona cried.

"I told you I don't know where the locket is!" Teagan shouted at the same time.

"Then think harder!" Maliya screamed back at her.

The vampires beating Venn pulled away. His eyes swelled, and blood dripped down a cut in his lip. His head lolled to the side as the vampires dragged him to his knees and forced him back beside me. I ripped my arms out of the vampire's grasp and caught Venn before he face-planted into the dirt. The vampires behind me quickly yanked my hands off him and separated us. They held on tight to my wrists, securing them firmly behind my back. I struggled against their hold, but I couldn't fight two at once.

"Let go of me!" I shrieked, but it was no use. All I wanted was to reach out for Venn and pull him into my arms.

"Stop it, or you're next!" Maliya threatened.

I continued to struggle and got one hand free, but it was instantly restrained again in less than a second.

"She means it, Rae," Venn groaned.

I stopped struggling, not because I knew Venn was right, but because I didn't know why I was struggling in the first place. Even if I managed to get free, I couldn't save Venn—or anyone else, for that matter.

"Guess again," Maliya demanded of Teagan.

"I don't know!" Teagan repeated. "Try the top drawer in the dining room hutch."

"No!" Fiona objected immediately. "I was just in those drawers. The locket isn't there."

Maliya raised an eyebrow. "Any other guesses?"

Teagan drew in shallow breaths. "Go to hell."

Maliya scoffed. "Honey, I've been planning my trip to hell for decades. It'll be a blast. In the meantime, let's see what kind of hell I can make for you."

Maliya gestured to the men behind me. Before I knew what was happening, pain blasted through the side of my head. I caught myself a moment before my face smashed into the ground.

Screams filled the air around me, but I couldn't make sense of who was saying what.

Stop it!

You don't need to do this!

Hit her again.

That last one, I was certain was Maliya, but it barely sounded like her over the ringing in my ears.

"Stop! I have another guess." I thought for sure that was Teagan.

Fingers tangled in my hair and yanked my head back. The hand on the back of my head forced my face forward. It connected with the ground with a sickening *crunch*. A flash of red crossed my eyes, and hot pain spread across my nose. The breath left my lungs as foot after foot connected with my abdomen. I tried to protect myself by crossing my arms over my stomach, but the pain continued. Blow after blow after blow.

"Go check," I heard Maliya bark.

Everything around me faded. The sounds. The lights. Everything. All I heard was the blood pulsing in my ears. All I saw was the pitch black of the inside of my eyelids. All I felt was the fresh, tender bruises on my skin and the excruciating pain of a broken nose. Every inch of my skin the vampires beat ignited in sharp pains.

It will all be over soon, Rachel, I told myself.

As soon as the thought crossed my mind, I realized that I truly believed it. These were my last moments. And it honestly didn't bother me.

I closed my eyes, welcoming the pain. Soon, it would all be over. Soon, I would see my family again.

It'd been so long since I'd seen my dad's smile and felt my mother's embrace. I hoped it was nice where they were, that the sun was shining, that it smelled like my mother and tasted like my father's homemade apple pie.

I'm sorry I couldn't save you, Jenna, I thought, as if she might be able to hear me from wherever she was. I believed with all my heart she was still alive, and I'd failed her.

I hoped I was wrong. For once, I *wanted* to be wrong.

I didn't want to say goodbye to Venn or the rest of them. I'd enjoyed my time with them. They made me feel like I had a family again, if only for a brief moment.

The pain seemed to wash away. I hardly noticed it anymore as a positive energy consumed me. Whatever happened next, I was ready for it.

"Finally, we have it," a satisfied voice cut through my clouded mind. "Kill them all."

My stomach twisted. I couldn't have heard that right, could I?

It was one thing to accept my own death, but I'd be leaving this world with one regret. I'd let another family down. I hadn't been able to save them.

It's not over yet, a voice in the back of my mind said. *You still have time.*

The voice was right. Until my soul left this body, I still had a chance. *Venn* still had a chance.

I peeled my swollen eyes open. Two vampires loomed above me, still delivering blows to my abdomen in what felt like slow motion. Their faces contorted in anger. Did they even know what they were angry about? I felt sorry for them. They probably didn't know what love was. Their curse had stolen that from them, and now they were damned to eternal misery. It wasn't fair of the vampires to take everyone else down with them.

It took all the strength I had to move my lips and force my vocal chords to produce sound. Past the dry, scratchy ache in my throat, an incantation spilled out.

"*Ardeat ignis*." I repeated the phrase I'd heard Genevieve use to ignite her candles.

I didn't know what I was expecting, but I wasn't ready for the sight that unfolded before my eyes. Red and orange flames engulfed the two vampires above me. The blows against my abdomen immediately stopped as they both stumbled backward, screaming in pain. Heat from the fires warmed my skin, and the smell of burnt flesh filled the air.

The other vampires on the lawn all stepped back, their eyes filled with utter shock.

"What the hell?" Maliya shouted. "Help them!"

The remaining vampires on the lawn rushed forward to help put out the flames, but this wasn't any ordinary fire. This was a witch's fire—*my* fire—and it wasn't giving up that easily. All of Maliya's cronies lit up like they'd been doused in gasoline, the flames spreading rapidly along their skin. It only took moments for the fires engulfing the first two men to fizzle out as their bodies disintegrated into a pile of ash.

Maliya screamed, calling attention to the vampires inside the house. I lifted my head to see a small group of them rushing toward the broken window in the living room to make it outside as fast as they could.

I muttered the incantation under my breath a second time. All throughout the house, red and orange light danced across the walls as Maliya's men burst into flame. Soon, the curtains caught fire, and smoke billowed out the windows. Glass shattered out a window on the second story, and a man alight with flames jumped out of it, screaming. He was already reduced to a pile of ash before he hit the ground.

Teagan and Fiona rushed over to Ryland, who was just regaining consciousness. Venn's swollen face came into view. He touched me gently, making certain he didn't hurt me.

"Rae," he said in a rush, helping me sit up.

That voice. That beautiful voice. I loved the way he said my name—

I didn't get enough time to enjoy it before a strong hand grabbed the back of my shirt and dragged me to my feet. Something sharp pressed to my throat. I glanced to the ground where the vamps had tossed the dagger, but it was gone.

I swallowed, but the fear had completely left my body. Instead, a sense of victory washed over me. Venn and his family were free to make a run for it now.

"What kind of trick are you and your friends playing?" Maliya spat into my ear, but she directed the question at Venn.

He'd shot to his feet. Fiona, Teagan, and Ryland all froze on the ground behind him.

"Let her go," Venn demanded. "You have the locket. You got what you came for."

Maliya laughed. "You know I don't work that way. All of my men are dead."

"Then kill me already," I said in a calm, collected tone. Even I was surprised by it.

"I want to know how you killed them," Maliya demanded.

"You forget..." Venn said as he took a cautious step forward. "We have a powerful witch on our side."

"Sondra?" Maliya asked. "She's not even here. There's no way she could—"

Venn didn't let her finish. In a precise, calculated movement, he leapt and shifted mid-air. His teeth sank into Maliya's arm.

She shrieked and dropped the knife at my throat. Her hold on me vanished as she stumbled backward. I whirled around just in time to see Venn's paws slam straight into Maliya's chest. She fell to the ground, and her arm instantly shot in front of her face to protect herself. The sleeve of her dress rode up her wrist, revealing a scar in the shape of a *V*.

"Wait!" I shouted before Venn could snap at her again.

He hesitated. I rushed forward and grabbed Maliya's wrist as hard as I could. I pulled her sleeve down to reveal the rest of the scar. It matched Cowen's perfectly. It was the same mark that had haunted my dreams for years.

"You're Soulless!" I accused.

Maliya laughed. "Does that surprise you?"

Venn looked up at me with a questioning expression in his eyes.

I ignored him and fixed my eyes on Maliya. A new hope filled my chest. The chance I'd thought had vanished had resurfaced.

"Where are they?" I demanded. "The Soulless. Tell me where they're hiding."

Maliya scoffed. "I left them years ago. Even if they're where they used to be, what makes you think I'd tell you?"

My grip tightened around her wrist, so much that her teeth gritted in pain. "Because if you don't tell me, I'll do the same thing to you as I did to your men."

Realization crossed her eyes when it clicked that I was the witch Venn had been talking about. My fist cracked across the side of her face. Her head twisted to the side, but her expression remained stone cold.

"Tell me where they are," I repeated.

She pressed her lips together.

I took a deep breath and leaned down to Maliya's level. My hands clamped around the blade at her feet. In a flash, my arm swung downward. The dagger stuck from her thigh, and a piercing scream ripped through the air.

"Rae," Venn's voice came from beside me. He'd shifted back to human form. "What's this about?"

I turned to him. "My sister."

Venn looked shocked. "Why didn't you tell me the vampires who took her were Soulless?"

"Because I knew you'd never let me go after them."

"No, I wouldn't," Venn agreed. "It's too dangerous."

I knew he was right, but I still burned to know where my sister had been the last two years.

"I need to know," I whispered.

"You'll just kill me," Maliya accused.

"I won't," I promised. It was worth letting her go if it restored my hope. I ripped the blade from her thigh, and she winced, biting back another scream. "But I have every intention of doing so if you don't talk."

Maliya's lips tightened, like she wasn't sure whether she believed me. "They're on Gregor Island," she admitted. "It's an island in the Great Lakes where Valkas served his prison sentence. It's been cloaked by magic for ages."

"How do I know you're not lying?" I asked.

Maliya smirked. "Because I'd like to see you try to take them on. And because I value my life."

As evil as Maliya was, something told me she wasn't bluffing.

Satisfied, I stood. "You know, you should really learn to read the contract."

"What do you mean?" Maliya snarled.

"I said *I* wouldn't kill you. I made no promises about you making it out of here alive."

I turned to Venn and stuck the handle of the dagger out to him. He glanced down at it momentarily and then took it. Maliya was Venn's demon. It was up to him to decide her fate.

"Wait!" Maliya cried, her voice shaking. She looked up at me with fear glistening in her eyes. "Who *are* you?"

"You know who I am," I said with a smirk. "I'm the Ravenite, bitch."

I turned away. Fiona reached an arm out toward me, and I slid mine around her shoulder. Teagan, Ryland, Fiona, and I faced the house, watching in sorrow as the flames consumed it.

A moment later, Venn's comforting fingers laced in mine. I glanced down to see the locket in his other hand. Behind us, Maliya's dress lay in a heap on the grass.

The sound of sirens blared in the distance.

"I think it's time to go," Ryland said in a strained voice.

Another beat passed as everyone stared up at the house that was once their home. They would never get their house back, but at least they still had each other.

And now I had a family, too.

24

I wrapped my arms around myself, trying to ward off the chill of the night. I was exhausted beyond belief, like all my energy had been sucked out of me with a straw. We'd driven an hour outside of Nocton and stopped in the parking lot of a public hiking trail. It was far enough away from any towns that we could set the bones in Ryland's arm without risk of anyone hearing his screams.

At least, we thought he would scream. It didn't surprise me that he was tough enough not to. He'd bitten down on a rolled-up t-shirt to silence the agony.

"You need to get yourself a pain-relieving spell," he'd told me after I cast the spell to speed his healing.

"Nah," I teased back. "It wouldn't be any fun if you couldn't feel it."

Though the car had already been packed half-full before the vampires attacked, I'd never gotten a chance to retrieve my things from my apartment. Even if I'd had a pain-relief spell copied down in my spell book—which I didn't—I wouldn't have been able to use it.

I stood on the bank of the river not far from the parking lot we'd stopped at. I stared out across the water that reflected the moonlight. Footsteps approached, and I knew without looking that they were Venn's.

"Ryland's feeling better," he said in a near whisper once he reached me.

A light weight settled on my shoulders, and my arms suddenly started to warm. I pulled the sweatshirt Venn had offered tighter around me and inhaled the scent. It smelled like cinnamon—like Venn. He stuck his hands into the pockets of his jeans and gazed to the tall trees on the other side of the narrow, rippling water.

A sense of relief washed over me. "That's good. It'll take a while until he's back to normal. I've found that the spell only increases healing by about a factor of ten."

"I don't know about that," Venn said. "He says it hardly feels tender anymore. Maybe with your practice casting the spell you've gotten better."

"Maybe," I agreed. "How are you feeling? How are your ribs?"

I looked to him. In the moonlight, I could see that the swelling on his face had significantly decreased. Even my own tender bruises didn't hurt anymore.

Venn gazed down at me. "I'm feeling better. Tired, but better."

I cracked a smile. "Me, too."

"You should get some rest," he suggested. "Fiona's already curled up on the back seat."

I could really use some sleep, even if I had to nap in the grass tonight.

"Once everyone's ready, we'll grab some food and then

head to Matias's," Venn said. "It's about another three hours away."

Teagan had explained to me in the car where they'd found the locket. Ryland had been wearing it. When he shifted, it broke off his neck and flew beneath the coat rack in the hallway. The family had once again found their hope in getting Sondra back safely. I had my hope for my own sister, but at this point, I didn't know what to do with it.

A silence hung in the air between Venn and me.

"You're still going after her, aren't you?" Venn asked softly. "After your sister?"

I turned to him and wrapped my arms around his waist. My head rested on his shoulder. The warmth of his arms around me and his breath through my hair was unlike anything else. I could almost forget the world had gone to shit. In his arms, I felt safe. Everything felt perfect.

"I am," I whispered.

Venn's shoulder's fell. "Then I'm going with you."

Relief washed through me, even though I knew it was selfish of me to want him to come.

I sighed. "I don't know where to start. The Great Lakes are *huge*. We need to narrow it down."

"I think Sondra might be able to help," Venn said. "She may at least know someone who can point us in the right direction."

I buried my face deeper into his neck, contemplating my options. "Then I'm coming with you. After we reunite your family, we'll reunite mine."

Venn smiled that heart-melting smile of his. "We will. I promise."

He bent down and brushed his lips against mine. My chest ignited with fireworks. A warmth spread over my skin, washing away the last of the tenderness in my muscles. I wondered if he knew he had that effect on me.

Times had never been worse, but they'd never been better, either. With Venn, I could honestly believe that things were about to change for the better.

Hang in there, Jenna, I thought. *I'm coming for you.*

END OF BOOK ONE

Continue the series in book two, *Resilience.*

ABOUT THE AUTHOR

Alicia Rades is a USA Today bestselling author of young adult and new adult paranormal fiction. When she's not dreaming up magical stories, she's either binge-watching paranormal TV shows, meditating, or spending time with her family. She has an unhealthy obsession with psychic characters and writes with a deck of tarot cards next to her computer.